About the Book

"Each one must live with his own conscience, Elizabeth . . ."

"No Van Swaenenburgh was ever a coward . . ."

Elizabeth van Swaenenburgh refused to listen. And she refused to allow the underground to hide refugees at Swaenenburgh Castle.

For centuries the medieval Dutch castle had been the Van Swaenenburgh family home. Now, in 1942, Hitler's troops occupied all Holland and Swaenenburgh was a German military headquarters. The German commander had promised that the castle would not be harmed—*if* the Van Swaenenburghs were cooperative. Elizabeth was determined not to risk the commander's displeasure.

But as the war continued and Nazi rule oppressed her innocent countrymen, Elizabeth gradually became aware that she could not remain aloof. She must find the courage to play her part.

Margaretha Shemin has written an exciting and suspenseful story that gives a sympathetic insight into the development of character under stress.

THE
EMPTY
MOAT

by
Margaretha
Shemin

COWARD-McCANN   NEW YORK

Library of Congress Catalog Card Number: 77–86301
Printed in the United States of America
12216

To Douglas, Barbara and Frances

Chapter One

SWAENENBURGH CASTLE was by no means the grandest example of medieval Dutch architecture, but to Elizabeth van Swaenenburgh, the sixteen-year-old daughter of the house, it was the most beautiful castle in the world and the only place where she cared to live.

The five-hundred-year-old castle stood outside the village of Swaenenburgh on a wooded hill, overlooking the gently sloping Dutch countryside. Two narrow bridges, one in front and one in back, spanned the moat and gave access to the cobbled courtyard. The wall that had once enclosed the courtyard had been destroyed by the French in the year 1673 and had never been rebuilt again. Crumbled parts of it still stood, overgrown with ivy and rambler roses.

The castle was three stories high with a stout tower at each corner. It was built of red brick that through the ages had mellowed into a soft, pale pink. There were many mullioned windows set back deeply in the thick walls and above the wide front entrance, carved in stone, was the coat of arms of the family Van Swaenenburgh, four white swans against a blue background, framed in gold.

Elizabeth sat hunched on her knees in the vegetable garden behind the house. It was a June evening in the year 1942 and she was busy pulling the weeds that were growing between the lettuce and radish plants. She should really help Jacob more often with the gardening. He was old and stiff with rheumatism and he had all the other household chores to take care of. She looked around the strawberry beds that needed hoeing, the raspberry and currant bushes that had not been clipped since their last gardener had left, and the apple and pear trees that should have been sprayed early in spring. But this was enough for tonight. Elizabeth pulled out a last stubborn weed and regarded with satisfaction the neat row of lettuce heads.

She got up, stretched and walked down to the drawbridge over the moat. Leaning over the side of the bridge, she looked into the water. The moat seemed empty without the swans.

There had always been swans at Swaenenburgh, from the day that Frank van Swaenenburgh, the founder of the house, had brought them when he had completed building the castle in the year 1442. The swans lived in the moat that surrounded the house and gardens, swimming silently and white through its deep, dark water. In the spring they built their nests among the ivy and roses of the ruined wall and on warm summer evenings the grayish brown cygnets, tired after a long day, rode around sitting on their mothers' backs. In the winter, when the moat was frozen and children came up from the village to skate, part of the water was roped off and kept open for the swans. Unlike most swans, these were a proud but gentle breed, because nobody had ever harmed them. Except for an occasional stranger, who might pilfer one of the nests in spring, no villager would think of bothering the swans. The prophecy, attributed to Frank van Swaenenburgh, was still believed in the village that harm would befall the castle, the village and the nearby monastery when the swans no longer inhabited the moat.

This spring for the first time in five hundred years there would be no swans in the moat and Frank van Swaenenburgh's prophecy seemed all too true, Elizabeth thought. She eyed the moat with distaste. The

9

water lilies were in bloom and floated with lovely disdain among broken bottles, twisted cans and other garbage that the soldiers had dumped there earlier in the day. Certainly nothing but bad had happened since the last swan had gone.

The birds had been driven away beginning last year, in the second summer of the German occupation of Holland, when part of the castle had been taken over by the military commander of the village. The incessant noise of soldiers, milling around and shouting in the courtyard, and of army trucks rattling over the narrow drawbridge had made most of the swans seek shelter elsewhere, but a few of the older and braver ones had stayed on. Elizabeth remembered the exact day and hour when they had gone too.

It was a late summer afternoon and she was standing at the window of the library, in the right back tower. Earlier, Jacob and her father had gone out, but she expected them home any time now. A group of soldiers was down below in the courtyard. For sport they were shooting in the air, scaring the swans. She could hear them laugh as they watched the confused birds swim around in tight, little circles, bumping into each other.

Elizabeth felt like running down and asking the soldiers to stop, but the thought of having to go amid these rowdy, big men scared her. She was never at ease with strangers and she was sure that by the time she had ventured among them she would be tongue-tied with fear and they would only make fun of her too. She hoped that her father and Jacob would come back soon.

Two swans who had got out of the moat were engaged in a furious fight and feathers were flying. Some soldiers close by were hissing and yelling, exciting the birds still more. Elizabeth could not bear to watch their cruel game. Oh, why didn't Father and Jacob come and do something to help the swans? They had promised to be home hours ago.

The only bird that had remained calm and unruffled in spite of the soldiers' tormenting was the big, old cob. He was Elizabeth's favorite swan. He was so tame that he would come up to her whenever she called him, and eat from her hand. Now he was swimming in the moat, his small, proud head held high atop his long, slender neck. One of the soldiers placed his finger on the trigger of his rifle.

"Stop it!" Elizabeth yelled. She could not bear to see her swan hurt. She rushed downstairs, out the back door and across the courtyard to the front, where the soldiers were, but the soldier had already pulled the trigger. She came just in time to see him scoop the mortally wounded bird out of the water. He watched the

11

swan for a moment, its breast heaving, then expertly wrung its neck.

"Ever had swan for dinner, Herr Major?" another soldier called to the commander, who was standing and watching. "It's supposed to be quite tasty, although this one looks like a tough old bird."

Elizabeth, completely forgetting her habitual shyness, ran straight up to the soldier holding the dead cob. She grabbed his arm and shook it roughly.

"You!" she yelled breathlessly. "You miserable lout, how dare you kill my swan?"

The soldier, a big, clumsy boy, his thick fingers around the bird's broken neck, stared in surprise at Elizabeth. She was a small, quiet girl, much too mousy and skinny for his taste, but she had turned into a fury and was yelling at him.

"I-i-t's only an old b-bird. H-he would h-have b-been d-dead soon anyw-way," he stammered. "I m-meant n-no harm."

"You, then." Elizabeth turned to the commander. "Can't you control your men properly?"

"Freule Elizabeth." The commander's voice was formal and icy. "Let me assure you that I have absolute control over my soldiers. This perfect marksman was shooting with my permission." He smiled at the soldier. "You on the contrary have little business to be here and insult me and one of my men. You seem to have

12

forgotten our agreement." He looked steadily at Elizabeth and she felt herself shrink. What had got into her that she had dared to speak like this to the commander? "I am an easygoing man, but there is a limit to my patience. Don't try me too hard," he said softly and Elizabeth realized again, what she had known from the very first moment she had met the commander. She was terrified of him. And she had crossed him. It was the first and the last time, she determined. Never would she cross him again.

Yet there was nothing so obviously terrifying about the commander. He was rather nondescript: a spare man, neither tall nor short, with gray eyes and light brown hair that had started thinning a little at the top. Elizabeth estimated his age as anywhere from thirty-five to fifty. His manner was formal and she had never heard him raise his voice.

The first time she had met him was after he had moved into the castle, when he had sent an orderly to bring Elizabeth, her father and Jacob to him. He had been sitting in the middle of the drawing room in her father's leather chair behind the heavy oaken table from the dining room. It was a different room, with the furniture rearranged to give the impression of an office. The chairs were lined up against the walls. Frank van Swaenenburgh's portrait, a genuine Rogier van der Weyden, that had hung for centuries in lonely splendor above the frescoed fireplace was pushed aside to make room for a life-size photograph of Adolph Hitler in a gilded frame. The commander rose when they entered.

"Herr Baron, Freule." He clicked his heels twice, once for Elizabeth and once for the Baron van Swaenenburgh. He ignored Jacob, who was standing next to Elizabeth. Jacob had not been given time to take off his apron and his hands were still wet and soapy from doing the dishes.

"I am Major Schmidt." His hand pointed at the portraits on the wall. "You have some beautiful things here. I am a great art lover myself and it will be a pleasure for me to live in this house. I feel very much at home." He turned to study the faces of all the generations of Van Swaenenburghs that looked down upon them from their picture frames: Frank's ascetic countenance; the round cheerful features of his little son, holding his pet falcon on his arm; the proud and haughty face of Maria van Swaenenburgh, who had lived in the castle when it had been plundered and ravaged by the French; and all the others. His eyes lingered longest on the radiant picture of Elizabeth's mother.

"One evening, when we both have time, you must tell me the life history of everyone that's hanging in this room, but now let's talk business." Major Schmidt sat down and took some papers out of the attaché case

14

lying on the table. Since there were no chairs nearby, Elizabeth, her father and Jacob remained standing.

The castle, the major said, had been taken over by the German Army. Major Schmidt and his men were legally entitled to occupy all of the castle and turn out its former occupants, but because he was a reasonable man, he would allow them to remain in the servants' quarters in the back part of the castle, if they so wished. He and his staff would occupy the front part. He needed all the big rooms in the house, except the library, which was too inconveniently located in the right back tower. The large butler's pantry off the dining hall would serve the major as a kitchen. He needed the six-burner electric stove and would send some of his men over to get it. He was sure the servant, Jacob, could find a hot plate or some similar appliance to cook on. For the first time Major Schmidt's eyes rested on Jacob, acknowledging his presence. Jacob glared back at him, his watery blue eyes full of hatred. At no time would the major tolerate interference from the "Herr Baron" or any discourtesy to him or any of his soldiers. This applied also to the Freule Elizabeth and Jacob. Major Schmidt cast Jacob a second glance.

"I hope we can live together agreeably, Herr Baron," Major Schmidt had concluded. "We are both gentlemen and I expect we can act as such. However, if you or anybody in your house gives me trouble, I should be

15

forced, to my deep regret, to take retaliatory measures upon you and your home. There would not be a stone of Swaenenburgh left standing after we got through, Herr Baron." Major Schmidt had not raised his voice, yet Elizabeth was sure that this was no idle threat.

"Your well-being and the fate of your home lie entirely in your own hands." He stood up, clicked his heels twice again and told the orderly to see the *Herr Baron* and the *Freule* to the door. Jacob walked down after them.

Nicolaas van Swaenenburgh had kept a stony silence all through the major's monologue, but back in the kitchen he exploded. He was a tall, heavy man, with a florid complexion and a fiery temper to match. His thick, unruly hair was snow white, but his erect bearing and his lively gestures belied his seventy years. With a bang his great fist hit the kitchen table, making the glassware in the cupboards shake. He swore out loud.

"To think of having to share my house with that man." Nicolaas fell into one of the chairs. "I'd rather leave altogether. What do you say, Jacob?"

"Oh, no, Father, don't say that." Elizabeth had been utterly shaken by the major's threats, but she could not bear to think of leaving Swaenenburgh. She would rather do anything, obey any order from Major Schmidt, as long as they could remain and keep Swaenenburgh safe. "Please, don't leave."

"What do you think we should do, Jacob?"

Jacob thrust his heavy lower lip out and scratched his grizzled head.

"Say we ought to stay, Jacob," Elizabeth begged him. If Jacob would think it better to stay, they would stay, Elizabeth knew. Jacob was the only person her father ever listened to.

"Well, Mijnheer Nicolaas"—a slow grin spread over Jacob's face—"I'd say it might not be such a bad idea to stay. The major's presence would make a nice cover-up for some of our activities. His office is handy and nearby." Jacob's face creased with laughter. "You and I could pop in and have a glimpse in the major's papers whenever we felt like it and read in advance what he plans to do around the village and make our arrangements accordingly. I suggest we stay, Herr Baron." Jacob straightened his arthritic body and clicked his heels in mocking imitation of Major Schmidt.

"You old rascal." Nicolaas burst out laughing. "I had not even thought that far ahead. Of course we'll stay. I haven't felt so good since the time those damned Germans made me resign as a judge from the Court of Appeal. This will give me a great chance to serve justice again."

"It won't be easy for you though," Jacob warned.

"You have to hold your temper and curb that quick tongue of yours, Mijnheer Nicolaas."

It had not been easy. Standing on the drawbridge on this June evening one year later, Elizabeth thought of the hard times. The day, for instance, when the soldiers had dug up the rose garden her mother had planted, to make a rifle range, and the day the little cupid, who had been standing in the fountain on the front lawn for hundreds of years, had been knocked off his pedestal by an Army truck. Recently Major Schmidt had appropriated her father's choice wines and Jacob's prizewinning Leghorn chickens. Each time Elizabeth was afraid that her father would not be able to hold his temper. But he had managed to restrain himself and so they were still here and Swaenenburgh was still standing. Elizabeth looked up to the castle. From this distance and in the rosy glow of the setting sun nothing could be seen of the damage done all around. From here Swaenenburgh looked as lovely as ever. Elizabeth turned and made her way back to the house and to her room at the top of one of the towers.

Her room had formerly been one of the maid's rooms. It had only one tiny window and it was right underneath the roof. It was hot upstairs and Elizabeth opened the window as far as possible. She didn't want to draw the curtains, so she washed and undressed in the dusk. By the last light that came in through the

18

window, she packed her school bag, laid out her clothes for the next morning, and wound her alarm clock before she crept into bed.

Thunder woke Elizabeth. The curtains billowed out of the window, lightning lit up the small room and rain pelted ferociously on the pointed roof above her head. The luminous dial of the clock showed a quarter past three. She got out of bed to close the window. The curtains were drenched and she wrung them out before she pulled them in. The rain lashed into her face as she stood at the window. It was too dark outside to see much. Just the faint outline of the woods below was visible. In the next moment, however, when a streak of lightning crossed the sky, she could see clearly. Three shapes were hurrying over the drawbridge toward the woods.

Who were they and what would they be doing? she wondered. They could have come only from Swaenenburgh. They must be three of Major Schmidt's soldiers on patrol or whatever soldiers did in the middle of the night. The soldiers, however, never used the drawbridge in back and the zigzagging path through the woods. For them it was much faster to use the paved road that started at the front gate. Also they didn't look like soldiers. There was something furtive about their movements. Maybe they were off on a little spree

19

without the major's permission. Elizabeth stepped back and waited for a second flash of lightning. But when it came, she couldn't see anyone. The dark woods had swallowed all of them. She closed the window and stood wet and shivering in her thin nightgown. She decided to go downstairs and make herself a warm drink before getting back into bed. On her way down she would look in on her father and Jacob, and if they were up, she would tell them about the men.

Since Major Schmidt now occupied the master bedroom upstairs in front and slept in the canopied fourposter in which most of the Van Swaenenburghs had been born, Nicolaas slept on the sofa in the library. The moment Elizabeth opened the door she knew he was not there. Nicolaas was a noisy sleeper. The room was silent. The heavy draperies were drawn and the room smelled of stale tobacco. Maybe the storm had wakened him too and he had gone downstairs. Elizabeth tried to dispel her growing apprehension. But Nicolaas was not in the kitchen either. There was only one way to go now. Elizabeth passed through the narrow corridor off the kitchen that led to Jacob's quarters.

Jacob had had the same rooms for fifty years. His quarters consisted of a bedroom, bathroom and a large room that he had used as a combination living room and office in the old days. Now it was the sitting room for the three of them. Jacob's office, as they still called

20

it, was empty, and after knocking a few times on his bedroom door without getting an answer, Elizabeth went in. The bedroom was empty too. The bed had not even been slept in. She opened the door of Jacob's closet, where they all kept their coats. Her father's and Jacob's raincoats were gone and so were their south-westers and boots. The spare raincoat that Jacob used for gardening in the rain was gone too. On its peg hung a gray coat that Elizabeth had never seen before.

Could it be possible that two of the three men she had seen had been her father and Jacob? But who had been the third? Elizabeth sat down at the kitchen table. She was still cold and a little hungry too, but she didn't feel like going to the trouble of making a hot drink. She would get some apples from the cellar and eat them in bed while she waited for her father and Jacob to return. She took the flashlight off the hook and started down the deep cellar stairs.

The cellar extended underneath the whole house. It was immense and it looked bigger still now that the wine racks were bare. Empty vats and crocks for sauer-kraut and waterglass eggs were piled on top of each other in the four corners. Elizabeth bent down to take some apples off the bottom shelf of the apple rack in the far right-hand corner. To her surprise she noticed that the rack had been pushed aside, thus exposing what looked like a panel, but what really was the door to the dungeon below. On impulse she pushed the panel aside. She hesitated for a second. She had not been in the dungeon since the days she had played prisoners with her friends Roza and Jennie, and she had never liked to go there alone. She crawled through the opening, bent down so as not to hit her head and went down the long flight of stairs.

Although the entrance to the dungeon seemed to have been made for miniature people, the dungeon itself was unexpectedly large. It could easily have held twenty men. The ceiling was low, the walls were made of stone and there was a dirt floor. There was a not unpleasant smell of earth and water, but there was something oppressive and menacing about the room too. It was like being buried alive. A table with two benches made from crude pinewood was the only furniture. Heavy chains with ankle bands were spaced at regular intervals in the walls. The Van Swaenenburghs had been known in history to have been faithful friends and noble enemies, but they had obviously treated poachers and horse thieves in the same way as every other landowner in those days. Elizabeth shuddered.

As children, she and Jennie and Roza used to lock one another in the ankle bands and bet who could stay longest alone in the dungeon. Ten minutes had been Elizabeth's maximum, Jennie could stick it out for an hour, but Roza was the champion. She had once stayed there for six hours. Jennie and Elizabeth had finally gone down, fearing that maybe she had suffocated, but Roza had been as calm as ever, only mad at them for spoiling her record.

Before she left the dungeon, Elizabeth let her flashlight run over the floor and walls and over the table. Everything looked neat and orderly. A little bit too neat and orderly, Elizabeth realized. The surface of the table and benches was free of dust and the earthen floor had been recently raked smooth. Elizabeth could clearly see her own footsteps. The steps going up to the cellar had been dusted.

Back upstairs she went straight to Jacob's closet and took out the strange gray coat. At first glance it seemed an ordinary man's coat. It was shabby, there was a button missing in the middle, and it was frayed at the collar and sleeves. She was about to hang it back again when she noticed the few tiny pieces of thread at the upper left side. Something that had been sewed on there had recently been snipped off. She looked closer and discovered a slight discoloration on the same spot. She slowly traced the discoloration with her finger. She traced one point first and then another. She did not have to go any further. With a pang of fear she knew that what had been sewed on the overcoat was the Star of David, the yellow star every Dutch Jew had to wear. She thrust the coat back into the closet.

Lying in bed under her warm covers, she could not stop shivering and shaking. She wished she had never awakened. She was sure now that the three men she had seen outside had been her father and Jacob and the owner of the gray coat. She had known vaguely that her father and Jacob were connected with the underground, the organization that fought the Germans. She had never dreamed, however, that what her father had meant by "serving justice" was so dangerous. Hiding and helping Jews escape were very grave offenses. They must have kept the man in the dungeon during the daytime. As she lay thinking about it, Elizabeth became sure that this was not the first time. Insignificant, small things that had happened this past year occurred to her. Food that had disappeared too rapidly. Clothes of Jacob and her father that were suddenly missing. *They must be out of their minds to smuggle people in and out of the house right under Major Schmidt's nose,* Elizabeth thought in panic. Her father had no right to expose himself and the family to such danger. Why couldn't somebody else have hidden this man? Why did her father and Jacob have to risk their lives? They ought to be stopped before it was too late. She wished she had the courage to tell them to stop, but she didn't. Nicolaas' fierce anger was seldom directed against her, but there was nothing he despised more than cowardice.

She was a coward, Elizabeth admitted to herself. She hated danger and she could not bear to think of what might happen to all of them if Major Schmidt ever caught Nicolaas in the act of hiding Jews. She couldn't bear it either if Swaenenburgh were destroyed.

If Hugo were here, I could tell him, she thought as she had done so often during the past three years. Hugo would have known what to do. But her brother was far away. Hugo had gone to England with his Army unit after Holland had surrendered; two Red Cross letters were all they had heard from him.

The only person she could talk to was Eva, who lived in Amsterdam where she had a job as a secretary. Elizabeth would try to call her sister tomorrow. She couldn't speak freely over the phone, of course, but she could tell Eva that it was urgent. Eva had always come when Elizabeth needed her, but she never stayed long. She found Swaenenburgh dull and while she adored her father and sister, she had frightful rows with Jacob, who said she was spoiled and selfish. Elizabeth closed her eyes and tried to get to sleep. With luck Eva could be here by tomorrow night.

But sleep would not come. Probably because she had been in the dungeon or because she had found the strange gray coat, she had started to think of Roza and she could not get her out of her mind.

Roza Cohen and her father had lived in the village

of Swaenenburgh, and Elizabeth, Roza and Jennie had been an inseparable threesome ever since nursery school. Mr. Cohen had been Elizabeth's math teacher in the Gymnasium in the nearby town. In September, when Jewish teachers and Jewish pupils were not allowed in the public schools anymore, the Cohens had moved to Amsterdam. Mr. Cohen taught there in the Jewish school and they had to live in a restricted part of the city. Jennie and Elizabeth had gone a few times to Amsterdam to visit Roza. She had always waited for them outside the station, her eyes lighting up as soon as she had seen her friends. They had walked through the city, the way they had always walked, their arms linked together and Roza in the middle. The only difference was that Roza wore a star.

The last time they had gone Mr. Cohen had told them gently not to come back again.

"It's not safe for you here," he had said. "There are razzias every day. We will see each other again when the war is over."

Nothing must happen to Mr. Cohen and Roza, Elizabeth thought fervently. *Somebody must help them.*

Nothing must happen to her father and Jacob either. She and Eva had to stop them.

Chapter Two

THE NEXT MORNING was Saturday and only half a day of school for Elizabeth. All morning long in school and on the way home, riding on her bike with Jennie chatting next to her, she had thought about the best time to call Eva and what to tell her.

When she walked into the house, Jacob was still busy setting the lunch table in his office. The precious china and the heavy silverware that Jacob insisted on using for every meal contrasted sharply with the threadbare tablecloth and napkins. Nicolaas' seat at the head of the table was empty.

27

"Where's Father?" Elizabeth asked. Usually Jacob would have lunch ready and he and Nicolaas would be sitting in their seats, greeting her with a "What the devil kept you so long, Elizabeth? We're starving." The food rations, supplemented only by the meager produce of homegrown vegetables and potatoes, were sufficient for Elizabeth, but were totally inadequate to satisfy Jacob's and Nicolaas' huge appetites.

"Your father is upstairs, talking on the phone." Jacob fussily straightened the knives and forks. "He's talking to Eva. She called. About time too, if you ask me. She doesn't write, never comes." Jacob jerked angrily at an uneven corner of the tablecloth.

"Why didn't you tell me Eva was on the phone?" Elizabeth threw her school bag on one of the chairs. "I've got to talk to her." She dashed upstairs to the library.

Nicolaas was standing with the receiver in his hand, ready to hang up.

"Give it to me, Father." Elizabeth almost tore the phone from his hands. "Eva, are you still there?"

"Elizabeth, Father will tell you everything." Eva's voice was far away.

"You've got to come," Elizabeth hissed under her breath, hoping her father wouldn't hear. "I've something important to discuss with you. It's urgent." But already the operator's voice was breaking in.

"Time is up," she said. "Your party is gone, miss. Please, hang up." With a disconsolate look, Elizabeth put the receiver back.

"Cheer up, Elizabeth," Nicolaas said, smiling at her. He had apparently heard what she'd said. "Eva's coming. You'll be able to tell her all your little secrets tonight."

In the kitchen he told the news. His face was flushed and his eyes were sparkling. Not only was she coming, but she was staying for three months. For the whole summer, he said triumphantly.

"About time she pays us a visit," Jacob said. "She hasn't been home since Christmas. And don't you count on her staying three months, Mijnheer Nicolaas." He sat down at the table with Nicolaas and Elizabeth and handed them the bread basket. "After two days she'll be gone as usual." He looked with concern at Nicolaas' excited face. "Calm down, Mijnheer Nicolaas, and eat your lunch."

"You old sour prune." Nicolaas grinned. "You haven't even heard the best part. She's given up her job to get married in September."

"Married," Elizabeth cried. Eva was getting married. It was wonderful. She and Erik had finally made up their minds. Erik was Jennie's older brother, who was a physician and was in practice with his father in the village of Swaenenburgh. No wonder Father was so

29

happy. He had hoped for a long time that Eva would get sick and tired of all her other boyfriends, settle down and marry Erik.

"I've got to phone Jennie." Elizabeth was up from her chair and on her way to the telephone.

"Wait a minute." Nicolaas pulled Elizabeth back by the hem of her skirt. "I didn't say she was going to marry Erik." The happiness suddenly left his face. "I wish she were. This is another fellow. I didn't catch his name, but she's bringing him with her this afternoon."

"She's marrying someone else, not Erik?" Elizabeth repeated in disbelief. "Are you sure you got that straight, Father? You know sometimes—"

"She's marrying someone else," Nicolaas interrupted her curtly. Lately his hearing was not as sharp as it used to be. It was something he did not want to admit and any reference to it made him short-tempered.

"This fellow is a doctor too, a neurosurgeon, to be precise. If I didn't get his name, it was because Eva was jabbering away and I could not make head or tail out of what she was saying." The heavy lines in Nicolaas' face softened and he shook his head in good-natured amusement. "Love certainly does strange things to people. I never thought Eva could be nervous. She's always so sure of herself. She sounded almost scared I might not approve of him." Nicolaas' eyes were gentle as they always were when he thought or spoke of Eva.

"But I approve of him as long as he makes her happy."

"A neurosurgeon." Elizabeth was duly impressed. "He must be very clever and probably much older too. He sounds glamorous." Maybe it was after all better for Eva to marry someone who was older and very important in his profession, Elizabeth thought. Eva was so beautiful and she liked excitement and interesting people. Ordinary people soon bored her. It might have been hard for Eva to spend the rest of her life as a doctor's wife in Swaenenburgh. Erik, of course, was wonderful. He was intelligent and kind and handsome too in a sturdy, rugged way, but he definitely was not glamorous.

"Well, whoever he may be, he'll have his hands full," Jacob commented. "Eva's a little devil. I can't count the times I put her across my knee."

"You were always prejudiced against her," Nicolaas accused him. "From the moment she could talk back to you."

"And you've always been like putty in her hands, from the day she was born," Jacob retorted.

"What time will they get to Swaenenburgh? Let's hurry up with lunch," Elizabeth said impatiently. If her father and Jacob started on the topic of Eva, they would never stop. It was the only subject they would not agree on.

"They'll be here around tea time," Nicolaas in-

31

formed them. "They were already on their way when she called. They're driving up in his car. We'll have real tea this afternoon, Jacob, none of that ghastly ersatz. You will also have to make something decent for dinner for a change. Your usual concoctions won't do. I'll pinch a bottle of my wine from the major. This is a great occasion and calls for a celebration."

Jacob looked glum. "I happened to peek yesterday when the major was out. There's not too much good vintage left. The major drinks it as if it were water. As regards dinner . . ." Jacob shook his head in despair. "What a day that girl picked to bring a guest. The end of the week and we've used all our food coupons."

"How about a soufflé?" Nicolaas suggested. "Elizabeth and I will steal some eggs from your chickens. How many do you need and what kind of wine do you want?"

"A half a dozen of eggs, please, and some Rhine wine or a Sauterne," Jacob ordered as if Nicolaas and Elizabeth were going to the store. "And as long as you're at it, take some liqueur too, Mijnheer Nicolaas. I'll serve liqueur and coffee for dessert."

"Off we go, my girl." Nicolaas put his cap jauntily on the back of his head. His eyes twinkled with the joke that he, Nicolaas, Baron van Swaenenburgh, former justice of the Court of Appeal, had become a very cunning thief.

Elizabeth dreaded these escapades, but her father did not tolerate any protest. She followed Nicolaas meekly across the cobbled courtyard to the large hen house beyond what had once been the rose garden.

This was the hour for rifle practice. Nicolaas had to duck behind the tall privet hedge that separated the soldiers on the rifle range from the path. Elizabeth walked close behind her father.

"You get in," Nicolaas whispered to Elizabeth. "Here, put the eggs in my cap. I'll call you if anyone's coming. Take the eggs from Annabel and Mirabel. They won't give you any trouble."

Elizabeth unlatched the door and slipped inside. The chickens were sitting on their bars, looking sleepily around. Annabel and Mirabel were sitting next to each other at the far corner. She deftly slid her hand underneath their warm, feathery bodies. One, two, three, four, five, six. Elizabeth's hand groped around till she had gathered the required number.

"Good girls," she whispered to them and tiptoed back to her father.

"Here you are." Elizabeth handed her father the capful of eggs. With one quick flip, that no experienced egg poacher could have improved upon, Nicolaas planted the cap squarely on his head. Elizabeth looked down at her dress to make sure there were no chicken feathers on it, and braced herself for the trip back.

33

"Just act as if we've been for a walk." Nicolaas nodded encouragingly at his daughter before he went ahead of her along the privet hedge.

When they emerged into the courtyard, there was Major Schmidt's car standing right at the entrance of the path. Major Schmidt was sitting beside his chauffeur, and as soon as he saw them, he jumped out.

"Herr Baron, Freule. What a lovely afternoon." His eyes scanned Elizabeth and Nicolaas. "You've been taking a little stroll? I saw you come from behind the hedge."

"Just a walk around," Nicolaas answered pleasantly. "To see how the water lilies are coming along. Good afternoon to you, Commander."

"Wait a minute, Herr Baron." Major Schmidt placed himself in front of Nicolaas. "I have a little problem and I think you may be able to help me." Major Schmidt paused. "Either the chickens are not laying so well or somebody is stealing the eggs." His tone of voice was pleasant, but his eyes had taken on the steely look that Elizabeth had come to fear. "Which of the two is it, Herr Baron?"

"I'm no expert on chickens." Nicolaas appeared unruffled. "But offhand I would say your first suggestion is right. Chickens being females are temperamental creatures, I guess. Sometimes they lay well; sometimes they don't."

"I would like you to show me the contents of your pockets, Herr Baron," Major Schmidt said formally.

"Feel free to search, Commander." Nicolaas looked at the major with the same stern expression that had made him one of the most feared and respected judges.

Major Schmidt's practiced hands ran over Nicolaas' sides. His pale face reddened visibly and he pressed his thin lips firmly together.

"I apologize, Herr Baron." He made a small, formal bow. "Good afternoon, Herr Baron. Good afternoon, Freule." He got back into the car as fast as he could, gave a sharp order to the chauffeur, and off they roared through the courtyard and over the drawbridge toward the village.

Back in the kitchen Elizabeth sat down shakily at the table.

"That's the last time I'm ever going to steal eggs," she said. "He almost caught us, Jacob." But Jacob, totally wrapped up in the dinner preparations, didn't sympathize but urged them to get the wine and Nicolaas, pleased with the success of the last venture, was ready for the next. It was a golden opportunity to break into the major's office with all the soldiers on range and Major Schmidt himself safely out of the way. Nicolaas ignored Elizabeth's pleas and there was nothing for her to do but follow her father once more.

This time Elizabeth stood on the lookout while her

father unlocked the door of the wine cupboard and rummaged around to find a wine worthy of the occasion and Eva's favorite liqueur. Nicolaas had kept a spare key for himself just as he had kept every spare key when he had to turn over the complete set of keys to the major. Elizabeth started to think of what she should wear tonight while Nicolaas, carrying a bottle under each arm, inspected the room. He blew dust off the frames of the portraits on the wall and fingered his precious alabaster chess set. It stood, a game half played, on the major's desk.

Eva could be here in less than an hour, Elizabeth thought. Luckily she was wearing her new skirt with one of the blouses her sister had given her. Tonight at dinner she would put her white woolen sweater over it with her mother's ruby brooch pinned on the collar. Maybe her father would even allow her to have her first glass of wine.

At last Nicolaas was ready and they went back to the kitchen.

"I'm going to meet Eva now." Elizabeth quickly made for the door before Jacob or Nicolaas could set her another chore. She had done enough for them today.

Sitting on a tree stump on the edge of the woods, Elizabeth waited. For the first time it occurred to her that it was odd that Eva's fiancé could drive up in his

36

own car all the way from Amsterdam. Very few people were allowed to have cars nowadays and the ones who did wouldn't have enough gasoline to make such a long trip. She hoped he wasn't one of those people who bought on the black market. Nicolaas disapproved strongly of such transactions. When he had found out that Eva had bought dresses for herself and Elizabeth with black-market coupons, he had been furious and made her return them. Elizabeth still couldn't bear to think of her dress, a pastel blue that felt just right and had made her look less small and skinny.

It was such a relief to think of Eva being home tonight. With Eva lying in the other bed in the small room they shared, she would tell her sister everything as she always had. Elizabeth had been only three years old when her mother died and her first memories were all of Eva—Eva bandaging her knees after she had fallen off her tricycle, Eva holding on tightly to her when she was learning to ride her first pony, Eva's hands pulling her out of the water when she had fallen into the moat. Eva had always been right there beside her.

Elizabeth looked at her watch. It was almost four o'clock and they could come any time. She watched the road, and when she was tired of watching, she shifted her glance to the fields. They were yellow with buttercups. A flock of pewits rose up into the sky.

"Pewit, pewit," they cried, climbing higher and higher. Elizabeth followed them with her eyes till they had become mere black specks. She looked at the road again. Way down, at the bottom of the hill, a small cloud of dust approached slowly. It was a car and it turned into the dirt road. It came nearer and nearer. Elizabeth jumped off her stump and waved her arms. She could see Eva, her head sticking out of the window.

"Elizabeth." Eva flung the car door open and was out of the car before it had come to a stop. She threw her arms around her sister and kissed her.

"Oh, Eva." For a moment Elizabeth clung to her sister, enjoying their closeness, the smell of Eva's perfume and the feel of her silk blouse against her own face. She had to wipe some sudden tears from her eyes.

"Is everything all right, Elizabeth?" There was concern in Eva's voice. "You're not crying because Father is mad at me or anything, are you?"

"Of course not, you silly. Why should Father be mad at you? He's very pleased that you're getting married." Elizabeth hooked her arm in Eva's. "Come on, show me my new brother-in-law."

"I know it's kind of sneaky to spring Kurt on Father," Eva rattled nervously into Elizabeth's ear. "But I knew once Father met Kurt, he would like him and would not object to my marrying him. But the phone connection was so bad and I was afraid Father had not understood what it was all about. Pooh." Eva wiped her face. "I've never been so scared in my life."

"I don't understand what you're talking about," Elizabeth said. "What is there to be—" She stopped in the middle of the sentence.

A man stepped out of the car and was walking toward them. *It can't be true,* Elizabeth thought. It was impossible, a bad dream, and in a minute she would wake up. She took a deep breath. For one moment she had thought the man was Major Schmidt. He was about the same height and build and wore the exact same uniform with the insignia, indicating that he was a major in the German Army. But when he was near and took off his cap, she noticed the difference. This man had thick brown hair. His face was tanned and his dark eyes smiled warmly at her.

"Elizabeth?" he said and stretched out his hand. Involuntarily Elizabeth drew back.

"He's a German," she said stupidly to Eva. The man laughed a little apprehensively and said something to Eva in a melodious, soft German.

"Well, didn't you know?" Eva asked. "This is Kurt von Anhalt, Elizabeth. Kurt, this is my sister. Please, shake hands with him, Elizabeth."

Elizabeth turned to her. "Eva, what have you done? Think of what Father will say when he sees him."

"I told Father about Kurt over the phone and you

yourself just said a minute ago that he was pleased about my getting married."

"Well, he won't be pleased with *him*," Elizabeth said with vehemence. She still could not believe the enormity of it. Eva engaged to a German officer! "If you were smart you'd take him right back before Father lays eyes on him. He thinks you're marrying a neurosurgeon."

"Kurt is a neurosurgeon and a very fine one too. That he happens to be German is not his fault."

Kurt pulled Eva aside and talked to her so rapidly that Elizabeth couldn't understand one word. They were close together. Kurt's arm was around Eva's shoulders in a protective gesture, his face bent down to her. It made Elizabeth sick to watch them. Eva in the arms of a German! Like the cheap girls in the village who sold themselves for a few guilders to the German soldiers, Elizabeth thought miserably. She had always been so proud of Eva. Eva was so beautiful and so popular; she could marry anybody.

"As long as we're here, Kurt thinks we should go see Father," Eva finally announced. "They will have to meet sometime and now is as good or bad a time as any other. He'll wait outside and come in after I have talked to Father first to prepare him a little. I can handle Father, Elizabeth. Don't look so glum." Eva managed a brave smile. Elizabeth nodded dumbly. Noth-

40

ing, she knew, would be sufficient to prepare her father for Kurt.

Eva seated herself in the car. Kurt held the door open for Elizabeth.

"Step in, please, Elizabeth," he said courteously.

"I'd rather walk," Elizabeth mumbled. Nothing would persuade her to sit in his car.

"It's more comfortable to ride," he insisted.

"Come sit next to me, Elizabeth." Eva moved over to make room for her sister. "On the way we can talk. Over the phone this morning you said you had to tell me something very important. You said it was urgent. Please, tell me what it was all about," Eva begged.

"It was nothing," Elizabeth said hoarsely. "Something very silly. It doesn't matter anymore now." She turned and started to run up the hill. After a few minutes Kurt and Eva overtook her. She dashed off the road into the woods to get away from them and kept running blindly, stumbling over the tree roots and boulders in her way.

She had lost her sister. Eva was farther away from her than Hugo in England. Never would she dare to mention to her what she had found out last night. She could not ask Eva for help, for Eva could not be trusted anymore.

Chapter Three

ELIZABETH KEPT RUNNING through the woods as fast as she could. She had only one thought, to get home and be with her father and Jacob when Eva arrived. Only an hour ago she had been enjoying the beauty of the woods. The chestnuts were in full bloom with white and pink candle-shaped blossoms and the ground was a green and blue carpet of thick, springy moss with patches of wood violets. When she lifted her face, she could see Swaenenburgh, shimmering pink through the green haze of the birch trees. She pushed away the flowering branches and ruthlessly trampled the violets under her feet in her haste to reach the drawbridge.

The first thing she saw after she crossed the draw-bridge was Kurt's car, parked in the courtyard. Kurt was sitting on the grassy bank of the moat, throwing pebbles into the water. Without giving him a chance to speak, Elizabeth ran past him to the kitchen door.

In the kitchen there was bedlam. Eva had apparently just arrived. Jacob and Nicolaas were crowding around her, talking both at once, and Eva couldn't get a word in between them.

"So where is the fellow?" Nicolaas kept asking, hugging Eva. "You look beautiful, my dear, but right now I'm more anxious to see your fiancé than you."

"Go get him, Eva." Jacob had already said it twice. "The tea is ready."

"Oh, please, please, can't you just listen to me for a moment?" Eva said. "I have to explain something, Father, before you meet him." Eva shot an anxious glance out the window to where Kurt was sitting, clearly visible in his uniform. "We can't talk here. Let's go up to the library."

The library was Nicolaas' domain. The large furniture was geared to his size and taste and the books on the shelves that covered the four walls showed his interest in law, farming and hunting. As usual Nicolaas and Jacob seated themselves in the big leather chairs, Eva sat down on one end of the couch and Elizabeth on the other, leaving as much space between herself and her sister as possible.

"You'd better tell us what's on your mind, Eva." Nicolaas smiled. "I'm bursting with curiosity."

"Stop stalling for time, Eva," Jacob said. "I'm prepared for the worst."

"Kurt is a very wonderful person, Father," Eva began. "He's kind and clever. He comes from a very nice family and he's even quite handsome." Eva laughed nervously.

"So what are we waiting for?" Nicolaas interrupted her. "Go get him."

"It's just—" Eva stopped for a moment. "He happens to be German," she concluded. "He has really nothing to do with the Army. He's just a physician. He's never fired a shot in his life. All he does is operate on wounded soldiers." Eva was falling over her words.

"A German?" There was an incredulous look on Nicolaas' face. "How on earth did you get yourself mixed up with a German, Eva?"

"He lives in my rooming house." Eva said. "Of course, I never paid any attention to him, but then about eight weeks ago I tripped in the hall and I sprained my foot. He was so nice, Father." Eva's face was glowing as she remembered her first encounter with Kurt. "He helped me upstairs and put a bandage on my leg. I loved him right away," she added.

44

There would always be men around Eva when she tripped or fell, Elizabeth thought. But why did it have to be this Kurt? Why couldn't a Dutch boy have picked her up and bandaged her leg?

"That was a very unfortunate accident," Nicolaas said heavily. "You understand, of course, that nothing can come of this, Eva. It's out of the question."

Elizabeth almost felt like laughing. It was as simple as that. Her father had forbidden it. She should have realized that this would happen instead of getting herself all worked up over nothing. This was just another of Eva's harebrained schemes. There had been several others in the course of the years, but a firm no from Nicolaas was all that was needed to get Eva back on the right track. Elizabeth sat back more comfortably on the couch.

"I cannot tell Kurt that, Father," Eva's hands tightened in her lap. There was nothing unusual about Eva's protesting, Elizabeth thought. Eva always had a good try to get what she wanted. But she would give in. Nicolaas was as unyielding as a rock and once he'd said no, nothing, not even Eva's tears, would sway him.

"You will have to," Nicolaas said. "And if you don't, I will tell him. I'll tell him to stay away from you, and if he ever dares to bother you again, I will—"

"I will talk to him," Jacob interrupted. "You better

45

stay out of this, Mijnheer Nicolaas. You might get too excited."

"None of you will tell him anything," Eva cried. "You're going to meet him first."

"Eva." Nicolaas' voice was full of tenderness, yet firm. "I know what's best for you. Let me or Jacob deal with him. You go upstairs and lie down a little bit."

Eva made no move to get up, but planted herself more squarely on the sofa. It was not going to be so easy this time, Elizabeth realized. She and Eva usually obeyed their father promptly and only once before had Eva stood up to Nicolaas. It had not lasted long though and it wouldn't last long now either, Elizabeth was convinced.

Nicolaas raised his voice. "Perhaps you didn't hear me, Eva," he said with ill-controlled anger. "I said, go to your room." There was no tenderness left in his eyes as he watched his daughter. "From now on you will stay at Swaenenburgh, right under my eyes." He heaved himself out of the chair and went to his desk. "I'll see you at dinner."

"I am twenty-one," Eva said and Elizabeth could not help admiring her courage. "I am of age and you cannot force me, Father."

"What is that?" Nicolaas turned around in disbelief.

"You cannot take Kurt away from me." Eva walked up to her father and put her hands imploringly on his

46

shoulders. "He's the only man I ever loved and I want to marry him."

"He's a German." Nicolaas roughly shoved Eva's hands away. "I cannot allow you to marry a German. There's nothing fine or decent left in Germany. They're barbarians." He stood back and measured his words slowly. "And if you marry him, you'll never come back here again. Never. You can make your choice. It's him or us." His face softened for an instant. "Please, Eva," he said.

She'll give in now, Elizabeth told herself. *She must. This time she almost went too far, but now she'll change her mind and do as Father tells her to.* She watched her sister.

Slowly Eva lifted her eyes to her father. Elizabeth had always thought that Eva was the image of their mother, but it suddenly struck her how strongly she resembled Nicolaas.

"I will marry Kurt, Father," she said quietly. Elizabeth's first reaction was surprise. She was more surprised than angry. Eva had chosen Kurt above all of them, above her father and sister and above Swaenenburgh.

Nicolaas was taken by surprise too, but his anger was rapidly getting the upper hand. His face took on a purple color and two swollen veins started to throb at his temples. Suddenly he turned to Eva.

47

"You're a slut," he cried. "You're nothing but a cheap slut."

At that moment there was a knock on the door, and before anybody had a chance to answer, Kurt walked in. Elizabeth couldn't tell whether he had overheard Nicolaas' words or was aware of the tension in the room. If he was, he didn't show it, for he walked straight to Nicolaas.

"Baron van Swaenenburgh," he said in his pleasant voice. "May I introduce myself? I am Kurt von Anhalt."

Nicolaas' eyes were as hard as stones. He looked past Kurt, ignoring him completely. "Get out, Eva," he said with cold contempt. "Get out of my house."

Eva took Kurt's arm. "We'd better do as Father tells us to," she said. "There's nothing for us to discuss here." She walked out of the room with her head very high.

As soon as the door was closed, Jacob pulled Nicolaas' chair up behind him. Her father's face was strange, Elizabeth thought. There were deep blue smudges under his eyes as if he had not slept for days. He suddenly looked very old.

"Sit down, Mijnheer Nicolaas." Jacob eased Nicolaas into the chair. "Stay right here and rest for a while. Get me the robe from the sofa," he commanded Elizabeth. With infinite care he tucked it around Nicolaas. "Is

48

that comfortable, Mijnheer Nicolaas?" he asked. "Anything else I can get you?"

"No, thank you, Jacob." Nicolaas leaned back in the chair. "Just leave me alone for a while," he said. "I don't want any dinner, but don't forget to call me for the nine o'clock news." He closed his eyes.

Downstairs in the kitchen Elizabeth stared out the window. Kurt's car was still in the courtyard, but now they were ready to go. Kurt held the door for Eva, then got in the other side. They sat close together. Elizabeth watched the car go over the drawbridge. The top was down and Eva's blond hair was blowing in the wind. She did not turn to look back at Swaenenburgh.

Slowly Elizabeth walked into Jacob's office. There was the dinner table, set for five with the wine goblets of Venetian glass and the blue and gold china that was used at Swaenenburgh only for gala occasions. There were the tall candles ready to be lit. Suddenly Elizabeth reached over and took the candles off the table, then the goblets. She couldn't care less what happened to them. She never wanted to use them again, but Jacob made her slow down. He packed the dishes and glassware in boxes and carried them down to the cellar, where he put them behind a stack of empty vats, out of Major Schmidt's sight. He made Elizabeth roll the silver spoons and forks, decorated with the crest of the Van Swaenenburghs, in clean towels and he hid them underneath his underwear in the dresser. When they had finally taken off the white lace tablecloth and put the red and white checked cotton one on the table again, Jacob agreed with Elizabeth that it was chilly in the office and that it would be more comfortable for the two of them to eat in the kitchen.

To take the chill off the evening, Jacob lighted the fire. Elizabeth pulled up close to the small stove. She was so cold. She felt as if she would never get warm again. Because Jacob insisted and only to please him, she ate some of the salad and the soufflé and after a glance at her pale face Jacob poured two glasses of wine. Her first glass of wine tasted sour, much different from what Elizabeth had expected, but it brought back some warmth inside her. When they had finished eating, Jacob made coffee and soon the kitchen was filled with its strong aroma. Jacob closed the curtains and turned on the light.

"Let's play a game of crapette," he suggested. "We haven't done that in a long time." From the dresser he took two decks of cards and started to lay them out.

It was like long ago, before the war, Elizabeth thought. On the nights that her father had taken Hugo and Eva to a party or dance or the theater, she had been allowed to stay up late with Jacob. They had always played the old French game of crapette and Jacob had poured her a cup of coffee too with lots of sugar and cream in it. She tried to concentrate on the cards, but her mind kept going back to Eva. Jacob stopped her twice when she forgot to make a required move and Elizabeth laid her cards on the table.

"I don't understand Eva," she said. "Why did she do this? How could she choose him above us?"

"She loves him," was Jacob's simple answer.

"Aren't you even mad at her?" Elizabeth was annoyed with Jacob. She felt the tears come to her eyes. "I hate her. I hate her," she cried.

"I only pity her." Jacob picked up the cards and sorted the decks. "She fell in love with a man. There's nothing wrong with that, Elizabeth. But he happens to be a German and it's the wrong time in history for a Dutch girl to fall in love with a German. If it were not for the war, your father would have been delighted with Kurt." It was the only time Elizabeth had ever heard Jacob defend Eva.

They drank their coffee in silence. Jacob prepared a tray for Nicolaas, some leftover salad with bread and cheese and a cup of coffee.

"I'll go up now," he said. "It's only eight o'clock, but I want to see how your father is doing." He put a small bottle of pills and a glass of water on the tray. "Dr. Timmermans gave me these," he explained. "It'll make him sleep tonight. Too much excitement is bad for him. But I just wish someone would tell me how to keep him from getting excited with Major Schmidt and Eva around," Jacob said with exasperation.

While Jacob was upstairs, Elizabeth washed the dishes and straightened the kitchen. It took Jacob a long time to bring the empty tray back, Elizabeth thought. Although the sink was spotlessly clean, she scrubbed it again and polished the gleaming faucets. She had just started on the stove when she heard Jacob come down.

"Elizabeth." From the tone of his voice alone Elizabeth could tell that something was wrong. She spun around.

"What's the matter?"

"Your father isn't feeling well, Elizabeth," Jacob said. "I called Dr. Timmermans. He's coming as soon as possible."

"What's the matter with him?" Jacob did not seem too alarmed, but he never called Dr. Timmermans unless it was something serious. For a cold or a headache after excitement, Nicolaas' most common ailments, Jacob had his own remedy, a stiff toddy, and Nicolaas preferred that to Dr. Timmermans' pills.

"I think he has had a slight stroke." Then to soften the effect of his words, he added that it didn't seem too serious. "His speech is somewhat affected and he can't move his right arm and leg. I am going back upstairs. You stay here and wait for Dr. Timmermans."

"Can I come with you? I want to see Father," Elizabeth said.

"Not now," Jacob answered.

"But if he's sick, I want to be with him," Elizabeth insisted.

"You know how much your father hates to be sick and helpless." Jacob spoke with his usual authority. "He wouldn't like you to see him in this condition. You can see him tomorrow when he's feeling better." Jacob had gone before Elizabeth could ask him more questions.

A stroke. To Elizabeth's mind came the picture of a pitiful creature who stared at you with vacant eyes, unable to move or speak. But no, she told herself firmly, there was no reason to think of her father like that. Jacob had said that it didn't seem too serious. She turned off the light so that she could see out the window, her ears tuned to hear the sound of the doctor's car.

But instead of the asthmatic puff of Dr. Timmermans' old Renault chugging up the hill, she heard the powerful roar of a motorbike, and before she had a chance to open the door for him, Erik stood in the kitchen.

"Oh, Erik." Elizabeth ran to him and threw her arms around his neck. She had never been so glad to see him as she was now.

"Hey, you're choking me," Erik chided her gently,

but he held her very tight himself. "Father is out on a delivery, but he'll be here as soon as he can get away. Meanwhile, he told me to have a look at your father." Erik took off his leather coat. He dug the stethoscope out of his bag and warmed the metal piece in his hands.

"This has been a terrible day for all of us, Elizabeth," he said simply. "No wonder your father got sick."

"Do you know about Eva?" Elizabeth asked.

"Yes, she called me this morning." Erik kept rubbing the stethoscope. Then he slammed the bag closed and ran up the stairs, two at a time.

There was nothing Elizabeth could do now but wait. She made a fresh pot of coffee, recklessly using the last coffee beans. The coffee was just ready when Jacob and Erik came down again.

"Your father has suffered a stroke," Erik affirmed Jacob's diagnosis. "He will undoubtedly get well, but it may take a long time, Elizabeth." He looked at his watch. "I want to wait till Father gets here, and see what he says, but I'm sure he'll agree with me."

"How is he"—Elizabeth searched for the right word —"affected?"

"His right side is weak," Erik said. "But the main trouble is that he can't speak. He understands what we say, though, and that's a hopeful sign."

"Will he ever be able to talk again?" At this moment

54

it seemed to Elizabeth she wanted nothing more than to hear her father roar.

"Of course," Erik reassured her. "In time. Meanwhile, you and Jacob have to see to it that he keeps quiet. Nothing must upset him. He will get well again, Elizabeth," Erik said when he saw Elizabeth was not quite convinced. "Your father is a man of iron."

Yes, Elizabeth thought. Her father was a man of iron. Nothing, neither Major Schmidt with his threats nor anybody else, had ever been able to break him, but Eva had.

While they waited for Dr. Timmermans, Erik talked with Jacob about Nicolaas' care and Elizabeth sat quietly, listening. Her father's nursing would fall completely on Jacob's shoulders, she realized. Jacob had taken instant charge of the sickroom and he would not allow anybody, not even herself, to take care of Nicolaas.

Jacob loved to nurse and he was marvelous at it. Elizabeth thought of the times she and Eva had had chicken pox and measles together. Jacob had nursed them with loving gruffness, and as she looked back on those times, they seemed like fun. She and Eva had always done everything together, Elizabeth thought miserably. How would she ever be able to get along without Eva? She felt tired, too tired even to pick herself up and go upstairs. The warmth of the stove and the low voices of Jacob and Erik made her drowsy; she let their conversation pass by her, picking up a word here and there, but not grasping the whole of what they were saying. She was on the threshold of sleep when the word "dungeon" hit her with full force. Instantly Elizabeth was wide-awake.

Jacob and Erik had pulled their chairs away from the table. Huddled together like conspirators, they were whispering to each other, but not so low that Elizabeth could not hear them.

"It has all been arranged," Jacob was saying. "They'll bring him here tonight and he'll stay till he can go down to the monastery in the village. We'll hear from Father André as soon as he can have him."

"Are you sure you should carry on alone, Jacob?" Erik asked.

"Of course," Jacob said. "Mijnheer Nicolaas would want me to. It would be like letting him down if I didn't."

"What are you two talking about?" Elizabeth's question took Jacob and Erik by surprise.

"Nothing. Go upstairs, Elizabeth," Jacob said.

"I heard everything you said." While she had listened, Elizabeth had experienced the same fear as last night, but now she could do something about it. And she knew very well who was expected. Another Jewish

56

refugee. "Nobody is coming tonight, Jacob," she said clearly. "Not tonight and not any other night."

"You've been dreaming," Jacob said gruffly. "Get to bed, Elizabeth."

"I woke up last night," Elizabeth continued. "I saw you and Father outside with another man and I found his coat in the closet. I could still see where his star had been. You're not going to hide anybody in this house tonight, Jacob."

"Nobody will find him, Elizabeth," Erik said. "He's safe here. Major Schmidt doesn't know there is a dungeon. Your father and Jacob have done it a hundred times and nothing will happen. You can't turn this man away. He has no place to go."

"And you told me just a while ago to keep all excitement from Father. You know how dangerous it is to hide Jews," Elizabeth said.

Jacob stood up to fill the coffee cups once more. "Your father would get far more excited if he knew we had turned away somebody who needed our help."

"Jacob is right, Elizabeth," Erik said. Elizabeth knew too that Jacob was right, but she was not going to give in.

"You'd better find him another place, because he's not coming here," she said stubbornly.

"You have no right to do this, Elizabeth." Erik

pointed his coffee spoon accusingly at Elizabeth. "If the Germans find this man, they'll kill him."

"And if Major Schmidt finds him here, he will send us all to prison and he'll destroy Swaenenburgh."

"You have no right . . ." Erik began again.

"Oh, yes, I have every right," Elizabeth shouted, losing her temper. She was frightened. How could she make them listen to her? What if they brought the man here against her wishes and what if Major Schmidt found him? "I forbid you to hide anyone in the dungeon," she cried. "You are not going to endanger our lives and my home for some unknown people in trouble." She was still not sure, however, that they would do as she asked them and she used her last weapon, the only argument she knew Jacob would respect.

"Hugo is gone and Eva is gone and Father. . . ." She had to swallow a few times. "I am the only Van Swaenenburgh left, and as long as Father is sick, I am in charge of Swaenenburgh."

"No Van Swaenenburgh was ever a coward," Jacob said with contempt.

Chapter Four

"As LONG as my father is sick, I'm in charge of Swaenenburgh," Elizabeth had told Jacob and Erik the night
Nicolaas had his stroke, and she repeated those same
words the next morning when she spoke with Major
Schmidt.

"I hope the Herr Baron will get well soon. Meanwhile, it will be a pleasure and a privilege to deal with
such a charming young lady." Major Schmidt bowed
formally. "However, war is war," he continued. "You
also must comply with my rules, Freule Elizabeth, or
the consequences for you will be very serious indeed."

"You will have no reason to complain about me."

Elizabeth had made up her mind to please him whatever the cost might be. If she did, nothing could happen to them or to Swaenenburgh.

During the first weeks of Nicolaas' illness, when Elizabeth was still in school, she didn't feel too burdened by being the mistress of Swaenenburgh. She held scrupulously to the rule she had laid down for herself. She did whatever Major Schmidt told her and gave him whatever he demanded. She didn't even protest when he took away their telephone. Luckily Jacob was too busy nursing her father to object to the way she was running the affairs of Swaenenburgh. But no sooner had vacation started than Elizabeth felt more alone than she had ever felt in her life before.

Jennie had no time for her. She was active in the underground and spent her days distributing news pamphlets that had been dropped from English planes, and doing all sorts of other things that made Elizabeth shudder with fear. She didn't want any part of Jennie's activities and she stopped going to Jennie's house and stayed at Swaenenburgh.

Swaenenburgh was not a happy place to be. Nicolaas' progress was painfully slow. Although he could now move his paralyzed arm and leg a little, his speech had not come back and he was apathetic. He showed no interest in his surroundings, which upset Elizabeth more than his muteness. She couldn't bear to see him lie on the sofa in the library, staring hour after hour at the same object in the room. Even Eva's letter telling them that she had married Kurt and would spend the summer with his family in southern Germany didn't arouse him. Elizabeth read the letter to him, hoping that it would make him angry or upset. She was willing to do anything that might make him respond. Almost anything. She still wouldn't do what Jacob wanted her to do.

"It's his helplessness that he can't accept," Jacob kept saying. "He feels useless, a burden to everybody. We can help him by showing him he can still be of use to our country." Jacob tapped with his foot on the kitchen floor. "Let me get somebody underneath here, in the dungeon, Elizabeth, and your father's spirits will improve."

But to this Elizabeth would not agree. She was angry with Jacob for trying to use her father to get his way. She was often angry with Jacob these days. Deep down, his words "No Van Swaenenburgh was ever a coward" still rankled. Also, now that the critical stage of Nicolaas' illness was past and Jacob had more time, he constantly questioned her decisions, and sometimes ignored them completely.

Jacob still took his eggs from Major Schmidt. "Your father needs them. He's as weak as a baby," was his argument when Elizabeth told him to stop. She agreed reluctantly. Nicolaas had indeed lost an alarming amount of weight and his pajamas hung loosely around his big frame. But she was frantic with fear every time she knew Jacob was on the prowl.

Thus the summer dragged on. Each day was the same as the day before. It seemed to Elizabeth that everything had come to a standstill, even the war. She had ignored Jacob's protests and given their radio to Erik, since they weren't permitted to have one, but she couldn't prevent Jacob from going to Erik every night to listen to the news. The news Jacob brought back was not encouraging. It was obvious the Germans would not be defeated easily and the way things were now the war could drag on for years.

It was still August when Elizabeth rode to town on her bicycle to buy supplies and books for the coming school year. At home she covered her books, sharpened her pencils and polished her old leather book bag. School would be a welcome change from Major Schmidt's demands and her constant squabbles with Jacob. So September became a beacon of light. If she could only make it safely till then, she thought, everything would be easier. All day long she tried to please Major Schmidt without displeasing Jacob too much, and before going to bed, she crossed off the day on her calendar with a big, fat cross. Another day gone. One day nearer to September.

But no matter how careful Elizabeth was, things happened which angered Major Schmidt.

It was unfortunate that Major Schmidt intercepted the mailman when he brought Roza's letter. Elizabeth was sitting outside, sunning herself, when he came around the house with his hands full of letters. There were bills, brochures and a large white envelope. Though her eyes were bleary from the bright sun, Elizabeth immediately recognized Roza's handwriting.

She stretched out her hand eagerly. She hadn't heard from Roza in weeks.

Major Schmidt turned Roza's letter around. "From Roza Cohen," he read aloud, emphasizing Roza's last name. He studied the address for a long time. "You seem to be very interested in this letter, Freule Elizabeth," he finally said. "Is Roza Cohen a friend of yours?"

He knew that Roza was Jewish, Elizabeth realized. He could tell from her name and her address in the heart of the ghetto in Amsterdam.

"N-no," she stuttered. "Only a very casual acquaintance."

"Keep it that way," Major Schmidt advised. "I don't approve of a Roza Cohen as a friend for a Freule van Swaenenburgh." He tossed the letter into her lap.

As soon as he had gone, Elizabeth ran upstairs to her room to read it. Roza wrote wonderful letters and this one was typical of her, filled with news about school, comments on books she had read and small, humorous things that had happened to her and her father. She described her new hairdo and had drawn a funny picture of herself with her hair all piled on top of her head. She had long black hair that had always been the envy of Jennie and Elizabeth. "You can see that I wear it now *à la* Cornelia," Roza wrote, referring to the portrait of one of Elizabeth's ancestors. "I think it makes me look like her, only luckily I'm a lot less ample." Not once in her letter did Roza mention the threat and the fear she and her father lived under constantly.

Elizabeth read the letter till she knew it by heart. Then she tore it up in tiny pieces, hating herself while she did it. Afraid, that's what she was. So afraid that she hadn't dared tell Major Schmidt that Roza was her best friend.

From that day Elizabeth was particularly careful not to arouse Major Schmidt's displeasure again. Still, on another day Elizabeth and Major Schmidt came to the point of disagreement.

It was an afternoon that Elizabeth had nothing, absolutely nothing to do. It was too hot to garden, Nicolaas was taking his afternoon nap and Jacob was busy in the house. Desperate with boredom, she had finally called Jennie, but Jennie had gone away for the day and would not be back till late that night. Elizabeth had finished two books and was not in the mood for reading anymore. She took her chess set outside and set up the board on a table under one of the big trees. She would play against herself. But it was not much fun and she was just about to gather the pieces back into the box and take the set upstairs, when Major Schmidt strolled by.

"Freule Elizabeth, allow me." Major Schmidt sat down on a chair. "You play chess?" He was amazed and delighted. "But you can't play chess all by yourself. I'd like to have a game with you."

"Oh, no." Elizabeth hurriedly put the pieces into the box. "I have no time," she said, clutching the box in one hand and picking up the board with the other.

"If you have no time now, then we'll play tonight," Major Schmidt said. "Is eight o'clock convenient for you? We can play once a week if you like. Back home in Germany I always played once a week."

"But I don't want to play." Elizabeth was so horrified at this suggestion that she forgot to be diplomatic.

"Are you trying to tell me that you don't want to play with me, Freule Elizabeth?" Major Schmidt said softly, but his eyes were angry.

Elizabeth was frightened and flustered. "I mean I can't. I play very badly. I'm sure you're much too good—"

"Tonight at eight in my room," Major Schmidt broke in. "I expect that will suit you, Freule Elizabeth." Elizabeth nodded dumbly.

When he asked her again the next week, she didn't dare refuse him and from then on the weeks went from Thursday to Thursday. Every Thursday was a fresh ordeal.

Elizabeth could not get used to seeing Major Schmidt sit in her father's chair with Hitler's face above him and strut around their room, fingering Nicolaas' most beloved possessions. The portraits on the walls were Major Schmidt's favorite topic of conversation. He questioned her constantly about her ancestors and he liked the portrait of the last Baroness van Swaenenburgh best of all.

"A very beautiful woman," he remarked, looking at Elizabeth's mother with the proud eye of the possessor. Elizabeth turned her chair so that she sat with her back to the portrait, facing instead the oil painting of Maria van Swaenenburgh. She had never cared for her cold, proud beauty before, but now it gave her strength. Maria had known war too, Elizabeth thought, and she was the only one in the room who would have understood exactly how Elizabeth was feeling.

She crossed off every Thursday on her calendar with an extra-fat line. Once school started, maybe, she could excuse herself some Thursdays without insulting Major Schmidt.

When the first day of school finally came, it was a splendid, sunny day and even the fact that it happened to be Thursday could not dampen Elizabeth's spirits. She cycled through the woods at high speed and the bumps in the road gave her the same sense of exhilaration she had felt as a small girl, jolting up and down in the back seat of Jacob's bicycle. The air was fresh and pungent and the woods smelled of fall, although the trees were as green as if it were summer. A full fifteen minutes early, Elizabeth reached the signpost on the highway.

Every day, rain or shine, for the past five years she had waited here for Jennie and Roza and together they had ridden the five miles to school. Last year had been the first year without Roza. Elizabeth looked down the highway. She didn't want to think of Roza. Today was the day she had waited for so long. Today was going to be a perfect day.

In school there were two new teachers, and although no official mention was made of it, everybody soon knew that one of the old teachers had been sent to prison for working with the underground. The other had gone into hiding.

With the exception of the new teachers, everything was exactly as Elizabeth had hoped it would be. War or no war, school was always the same, she thought happily. She and Jennie picked seats next to each other as they had for years. French was dull as usual, the English period was still disorderly and the Latin teacher was more sarcastic than ever. Elizabeth enjoyed every moment of it. The barren schoolroom with its walls badly in need of paint was like a protective shell around her. Through the high, old-fashioned windows the noises of the street came as from another world and the airplanes that flew overhead made no more noise than a buzzing bee. Here in school the war seemed far away. Here she was not the mistress of Swaenenburgh with all the awesome responsibilities that came with it, but just Elizabeth, a girl who had nothing to fear if she did as the teacher told her. For the first time since her father's illness Elizabeth felt safe.

On the way home the glowing feeling of safety stayed with her. For once Jennie did not talk about her dangerous underground exploits. They rode slowly, enjoying the sunshine, chattering about homework and the new teachers. Even the sound of an airplane flying over could not disturb Elizabeth's sense of peace.

"Look at that plane." Jennie pointed at the sky. "It's flying so low. Maybe it's going to drop pamphlets."

Jennie and her pamphlets. Elizabeth was annoyed. She gave the pedal of her bike an angry kick. All day long everything had been so wonderful, but no sooner did Jennie spy a plane than off she was again, talking about her pamphlets. She ignored Jennie's remark and continued to talk about homework, but Jennie was not to be distracted.

"It's really going low now. Maybe they're surveying the area." Jennie's eyes were fixed on the plane.

"It's an English plane." In spite of herself, Elizabeth was interested. She could clearly recognize the RAF emblem on the body and she was surprised that the guns from the nearby airfield had not already opened fire.

"He's pulling up a little." Jennie gave a sigh of relief. "I hope he'll get away before they start shooting." She had barely said the words when the earsplitting noise of the antiaircraft guns broke out above their heads. Elizabeth and Jennie threw their bicycles down and jumped into the ditch beside the road. Crouched on the side so as not to get her shoes wet, Elizabeth sat with her head in her lap and her thumbs pressed into her ears. It was as if the world around them were exploding. She felt Jennie nudge her side and she peeked cautiously at her friend.

"They got him," Elizabeth read from her lips.

The plane had lost one wing and was flying wild, diving down and rising again in a hopeless attempt to escape. It was an easy mark for the guns below, and when the ground fire hit again, it ripped off the other wing. Elizabeth and Jennie watched with horror as the plane hovered briefly above the trees before it came down, nose first.

But just before the plane plunged a hatch opened up underneath.

"I can't bear to look," Elizabeth said, but she did. The first parachute fanned out fully and sailed down unharmed amid the barrage of gunfire for a perfect landing.

"He made it." Jennie grabbed Elizabeth's arm and squeezed hard.

The second parachute did not open. Perhaps it had been hit or the parachute had been faulty to begin with. Elizabeth's eyes followed the figure of a man as it fell very fast from the sky. The guns stopped and suddenly everything was very still.

But the quietness did not last more than a few seconds. At the same time that they saw the man's body hit the ground the plane landed in a clump of low bushes. Instantly the bushes were ablaze and everything was shrouded in smoke and fire. On the road in front of them Army trucks and fire engines, which had appeared miraculously from nowhere, were pounding toward the fire. Elizabeth and Jennie waited till the worst of the traffic had passed before they picked up their bicycles and rode toward home. They pedaled the rest of the way without saying a word.

"He didn't feel it," Jennie said to Elizabeth as they were about to part. "Erik says that it goes too fast to feel any pain."

When Elizabeth got home, she found Swaenenburgh in uproar. The courtyard was swarming with soldiers and trucks. Major Schmidt strode amid the excitement, barking orders, and soon the trucks, filled with
heavily armed men, thundered over the drawbridge in
the direction of the village.

In the kitchen the excitement was as great as it had
been outside. Jacob was firing question after question
at Erik, who had just come in. He repeated for Elizabeth what he had heard in the village. One man, of
course, was dead, but the rumor in the village was that
the other, though wounded, had escaped. The soldiers
who had just left Swaenenburgh were undoubtedly a
search party.

Erik stayed for dinner and he and Jacob talked on
and on, making guesses about why the plane had been
flying so low and whether the wounded airman would
be found soon. Elizabeth tried to change the topic of
conversation. She didn't want to talk about the plane
anymore. It upset her to think of the man, falling so
fast. In her imagination she could see him tugging on
the strings of his parachute, tugging and tugging. To
forget, she began to talk about school, but nobody
wanted to hear about her first day in school.

Maybe Major Schmidt was too busy tonight to play
chess, Elizabeth thought hopefully. If not, *she* would
ask him to be excused. She had homework to do for

71

tomorrow. It would be lovely to sit upstairs in her room, with her books and papers spread out on her desk and forget all about the plane. It was close to eight when they finished dinner. Elizabeth decided to go up to Major Schmidt and tell him right now that she couldn't play tonight.

"Keep your eyes and ears open, Elizabeth," Jacob said as she was about to leave the room. "You may pick up some news about the missing pilot."

"I'm not going," Elizabeth answered.

"But you must," Jacob said. "Tonight you absolutely must go."

"You can't pass up a chance like this." Erik was appalled.

"Major Schmidt never talks about anything but chess and the art treasures of Swaenenburgh," Elizabeth protested. "I won't learn a thing from him."

"Go," Jacob urged her. "He won't like it if you don't show up on time."

Elizabeth still had no intention of going and she paid no attention.

"Major Schmidt is probably in a bad mood with the Englishman still at large," Erik said as if talking to Jacob.

"And when he's in a bad mood, he can make trouble over nothing," Jacob added shrewdly.

"All right, I'll go." Elizabeth reluctantly gave up a

quiet evening of homework. "But I'm sure Major Schmidt won't tell me a thing."

Elizabeth was right. Major Schmidt did not talk about the incident. He was tense, however, and kept looking at the phone as if he were waiting for a message. A few times he seemed about to get up, but he stayed at the table. He was an excellent chess player and he usually won, but tonight Elizabeth captured his pieces one after another.

When they had played for about an hour, it started to rain, at first softly, but soon rain was coming down heavily. A strong wind had come up and whipped tree branches against the windows of Swaenenburgh.

"*Verdammt*," Major Schmidt swore under his breath. He pushed the chess set aside with a savage thrust that sent Elizabeth's king and queen flying off the table. "It always rains in this damnable country." He walked with big strides to his desk and shouted into the telephone. Elizabeth was thoroughly frightened. She had often seen Major Schmidt angry, but never before had she seen him lose his temper.

"*Herein*," he called when one of the orderlies knocked on the door. Major Schmidt barked a torrent of staccato questions at him and the orderly answered, visibly nervous.

"*Jawohl*, Herr Major. *Nein*, Herr Major. *Jawohl*, Herr Major." *He's afraid of him too*, Elizabeth thought, and

73

she felt almost sorry for him. She bent over the chess-board and put away the pieces. She wished she had understood what Major Schmidt had asked the orderly, but he had talked much too fast.

"I'm coming myself." Major Schmidt put on his coat and cap. "Nothing I can leave to you," he shouted. "Nothing, not even the simplest order. Idiots you are, all of you." He scribbled on a piece of paper and handed it to the orderly. "Get this out instantly and tell the men I'm coming." He turned to Elizabeth.

"Excuse me, Freule Elizabeth, but we'll have to finish our game some other time."

When Elizabeth told Jacob and Erik about her evening with Major Schmidt, they were inclined to believe that the missing airman was still at large. This would explain Major Schmidt's outburst of temper about the weather. Rain and storm would make the search much harder. It would also explain Major Schmidt's fury at his men for not carrying out his orders properly. But these were only guesses. Jacob and Erik would spend the rest of the evening guessing, Elizabeth knew, but she had heard enough. She left the room. On her way upstairs she looked in on her father and, when she saw he was awake, kissed him goodnight. Then at last she went to her room to do her homework.

In her own room, with the curtains tightly drawn and the lamp shining on her desk, Elizabeth tried to recapture the happy feeling she had had earlier in the day, but she couldn't. Her mind kept wandering from her homework and it took her a long time to finish. She heard Jacob come up to make her father comfortable for the night and much later she heard Erik leave on his motorcycle. It was past twelve when she turned off her light. She opened her window and looked out. The rain had stopped and a full moon was shining over the deserted courtyard. Major Schmidt and his men had not yet returned.

Elizabeth slept fitfully and was instantly awake hours later when she heard Jacob call her name. He was standing beside her bed.

Elizabeth's first thought was that something had happened to her father. "What's the matter with Father?" she asked. She jumped out of bed and stood, dizzy with sleep, on the cold floor.

"No, no, your father's all right. He's sound asleep," Jacob said. "But you must come down with me, Elizabeth. I think I have found the missing airman."

"Found him?" Elizabeth whispered.

"There's a man outside," Jacob said. "I almost fell over him when I went to get some eggs. He's lying right behind the hen house. He's wounded and he speaks English."

A wounded man who spoke English. Elizabeth was

not at all sleepy anymore. She slipped a skirt and sweater over her nightgown and followed Jacob.

The man was lying facedown on the narrow path that ran between the hen house and the moat. He was in slacks and an undershirt. His clothes were wet from the rain. His right foot was turned at an odd angle under his leg and his shoulder was bandaged clumsily with a handkerchief, caked with blood.

Jacob and Elizabeth kneeled beside him and Jacob gently turned the man on his back. In the moonlight his face was greenish white, his eyes were closed and he seemed barely alive. Elizabeth wiped mud off his face with her handkerchief and the man opened his eyes, then closed them again.

"What do we do with him, Jacob?"

"You know very well what we'll do with him," Jacob said. "We'll carry him inside and put him in the dungeon. As soon as we've got him settled there, we'll call Erik. He's in bad shape." Jacob thrust his hands under the man's armpits and hoisted him into a sitting position from which he could lift him. The man groaned. In the quiet of the wood it sounded very loud.

"Hush." Elizabeth quickly covered the man's mouth with her hand. "I don't dare hide him," she said.

Jacob acted as if he hadn't heard her. "You've got to help me, Elizabeth." Jacob was panting. "He's a big man. Heavier than I thought. I don't want to hurt him more than is necessary." Jacob wiped his forehead. "You take his legs."

"We can't hide him," Elizabeth said over and over again. "We can't. We can't."

Jacob took his watch out of his pocket. "It's a quarter of two," he said. "The sentinel makes his rounds every hour. He'll find him in a little over fifteen minutes."

The man opened his eyes again and struggled to speak. "Water," he said. "Please, water."

Elizabeth put her hand on his forehead. "He's as hot as fire," she said. "He must have a raging fever."

"We're losing time, Elizabeth," Jacob urged. "We either take him or we don't, and if we don't, we'd better get out of here before Major Schmidt finds us."

"Water," the man repeated. "Please, water."

Elizabeth looked down at him. With his face smudged with mud and his hair tumbling over his forehead he seemed pathetically young and helpless. She thought of Major Schmidt's anger last night. Major Schmidt would not have any mercy on the pilot who, though wounded, had managed to elude him and his men for so many hours. By now Major Schmidt would be in a very ugly mood indeed. Elizabeth bent down to the man.

"You'll have some water as soon as we've taken you inside my house," she said.

Chapter Five

THE ENGLISHMAN was heavy and the distance they had to carry him seemed far. Elizabeth couldn't tell whether he was conscious or not. His eyes were closed, but his mouth kept twitching as if he were making a great effort not to cry out in pain. Elizabeth was holding him by the legs, trying not to touch the twisted foot, while Jacob was straining his short, thin arms to reach around the man's chest. The path on which they walked was strewn with fallen leaves and slippery from last night's rain. By the time they had reached the courtyard both Elizabeth and Jacob were out of breath.

"We must move faster," Jacob panted. "The sentry will be around in a few minutes." Elizabeth shifted her grip to get a firmer hold and the man moaned softly.

"Hold it right there." Jacob gingerly put his end of the body down, pulled a handkerchief from his pocket and stuffed it in the man's mouth. "Now, move," he ordered crisply. The man was like a lifeless burden between them as they crossed the open courtyard. Jacob opened the kitchen door and dragged him inside. Elizabeth had barely turned the key in the lock when she heard the slow measured footsteps of the sentry come around the corner. They had made it. She leaned, dizzy with relief, against the door. Her head was swimming.

But inside, they were still not safe. Earlier that night, when Jacob had gone for eggs, he had opened the curtains to survey the courtyard. Coming back, in his confusion over finding the Englishman, he had forgotten to draw them again.

"We've got to conceal him. Quick." Jacob whispered into Elizabeth's ear and together they moved the inert body across the kitchen floor and almost out of sight. Jacob took off his coat and folded it under the man's head. The sentry's footsteps came closer. Elizabeth and Jacob crouched down beside the man.

"We'll wait till he has completed his rounds before we go down into the dungeon." Jacob put his arm protectively around Elizabeth's shoulders and she could feel the itchy wool of his jacket against her cheek.

"He must have heard something. He's coming toward us." Elizabeth hugged Jacob closer. The sentry's footsteps stopped in front of the kitchen door. Elizabeth could see him clearly outlined through the glass. He was fumbling with his flashlight.

Jacob's horny fingers closed hard around Elizabeth's hand.

The sentry rattled the doorknob and a second later he shone his flashlight into the kitchen. The strip of light playfully jumped from the table onto the sink and down to the floor, missing the man's feet by a few inches. Elizabeth closed her eyes. She expected any moment now to hear the soldier bang on the door, but the footsteps retreated. For a few minutes Elizabeth and Jacob remained motionless; then the footsteps came back and passed by.

Jacob stood up and stretched his stiff legs. "We have exactly one hour before he comes around again," he said. "Let's get him downstairs." He pulled Elizabeth to her feet.

"He looks dead." Elizabeth bent over the man. "He hasn't moved at all since we put him down." She took the gag from his mouth and gently splashed some water on his face. To her relief the man gasped and sputtered.

It was not easy to get the wounded man down the

cellar steps, for he was in no state to help. As soon as they started to move him, he had become delirious, thrashing around wildly when Elizabeth touched the injured leg. Jacob decided to lay him flat on the stairs and pull him down. Elizabeth walked ahead with the flashlight, bracing herself whenever Jacob, unable to hold the man back, seemed about to fall on top of her. The man groaned every time Jacob pulled him down another step.

"I have to stop for a minute before we start on the dungeon steps." Jacob, purple and winded, let the man come to an abrupt stop at the bottom of the stairs. The man yelled out in pain.

"I better put the gag back in." Jacob stuffed the handkerchief into the man's mouth. "All right, here we go again."

"I'll give you a hand." Elizabeth picked up the man's legs again. She hated to hurt him even more now that he could not protest, but she knew that Jacob could never manage by himself. She helped Jacob move the man across the cellar, and when they reached the steps into the dungeon, they used the same technique to get him down.

The long flight of stairs spiraled toward the dungeon, twisting and turning. Elizabeth had always known the exact number of turns, but she soon lost count. The stairs were extremely narrow and it was hard to ma-

81

neuver the Englishman without bumping him into the rough stone walls. Every time her light showed yet another turn in the stairs she was sure that this must be the last, but then came another and another. The dank smell of earth and water grew stronger. Elizabeth felt as if she were in the midst of a nightmare, walking down a never-ending staircase, but finally the dungeon opened up at her feet.

"We'd better get Erik quickly," Jacob said as soon as they had hoisted the man onto one of the benches. "Damn Major Schmidt for taking away our telephone," he swore. "You'll have to go get him right now, Elizabeth."

"Me?"

"I'm afraid so." Jacob had taken the man's shoe and sock off and removed the dirty bandage from the shoulder. The ankle was swollen and twisted and the gaping shoulder wound, with the flesh around it blotchy and purple, made Elizabeth sick. She turned her face away.

"I'm afraid to go," she said. "There'll be soldiers all over searching for him. How will I get through?"

"You can tell them your father is sick and needs a doctor quick," Jacob said. Elizabeth still hesitated.

"Elizabeth!" Jacob exclaimed impatiently. "The man's almost dead and you stand there making excuses for yourself." His voice softened a little. "They'll let a girl through much sooner than me. That's why you have to go."

The man had been lying still for the last few minutes, but suddenly his body was caught in a fit of coughing. Jacob helped him to sit up. The man coughed and retched, unable to stop.

"He's choking," Elizabeth said. She was sure the man was dying and she could tell that Jacob was frightened too. He held the man as he vomited on the floor. His face was blue and beads of perspiration appeared on his forehead.

"I'll go." Elizabeth ran up the stairs.

Elizabeth knew every bush and tree, every zigzagging path and even the smallest clearing in the woods that surrounded Swaenenburgh, but she had never ridden alone through the woods by night before. The moon had gone behind the clouds and her eyes had to get used to the darkness. Although every inch of the path was familiar to her, the wheels of her bicycle kept bumping into fallen branches torn from the trees by last night's storm. She had expected to come across soldiers in the woods and she listened for their voices, but the only sound she heard was the breaking of twigs as she rode over them.

From the moment Jacob had awakened her till now, she had not had time to think about what she was doing. Now, riding in the quiet of the night through her woods, for the first time she fully realized the enormity of their deed. She who had forbidden Jacob to hide Jews in the dungeon was helping him to do something far graver. Hiding an Allied soldier was an act of sabotage. Punishable by death. The more she thought about it, the more frightened she became. He would have to go as soon as possible, Elizabeth decided. Erik must patch him up quickly. And this was the last time, the very last time she would let herself be trapped into hiding somebody in the dungeon.

As soon as Elizabeth came to the edge of the woods, it became easier for her to see her way. There was still no moon, but it was lighter in the open field than it had been among the tall trees. She rode faster. Down at the signpost where she always met Jennie, she ran into the first group of soldiers. They had barricaded the road.

"Your identity card, please." A big soldier, his gun drawn, stepped forward, but as soon as he saw she was only a girl, he relaxed. "What are you doing here in the middle of the night?" he asked, not unfriendly.

"My father is sick and I'm on my way to the doctor." Elizabeth didn't need to pretend worry. She was terrified that he would not let her through. "Please," she begged. "I have to get a doctor."

The soldier, realizing her genuine anxiety, called other soldiers over and together they argued for a while whether to let her through or not. Then one, whom Elizabeth recognized from Swaenenburgh, spoke up.

"Can't you see how worried and upset she is?" he said. "Let her go through." He gave her a kind smile as she passed by.

That had not been as bad as she had expected. Elizabeth coasted down the hill and was just about to turn into the main street of the village when a small Army truck overtook her, its horn honking. The truck stopped a little farther down the road and a soldier jumped out. What does he want? Elizabeth panicked. She pressed on her brakes and came to a full stop. It was the same soldier.

"I'll put your bike in the truck and take you down to the doctor," he said. "There are more roadblocks in the village, and if they don't know you, you might have a hard time getting through. Major Schmidt has given strict orders."

Elizabeth didn't like to accept his offer. If the circumstances had been different, she might have welcomed his kindness, but now he might be more a hindrance than a help. The soldier saw her hesitation and, not knowing its cause, interpreted it in his own way.

"I'm a father myself," he said. "This is no time for a young girl to be out alone." He lifted her bike into the truck and there was nothing for Elizabeth to do but climb in beside him.

"Your father had another stroke?" he asked. Elizabeth nodded. All the way he kept talking in a good-natured attempt to put her at ease. His name was Herman Geissler and his rank was *Feldwebel*. His daughter was a little younger than Freule Elizabeth, but much bigger, he added with pride. A real German girl with blue eyes and blond hair. Elizabeth answered *ja* and *nein* at random. When they reached the Timmermans' house, she thanked him effusively, in her eagerness to be rid of him. Feldwebel Geissler's broad face beamed.

"I'll come with you." He followed her down the path and pressed the night buzzer for her.

"Please, don't wait here with me. You have been very kind and I hate to take up any more of your time," Elizabeth protested. If there was one thing worse than a nasty German, it was a helpful German. How could she ever talk to Erik with Feldwebel Geissler present?

It seemed an eternity before she heard footsteps coming down the hallway. Erik, still tying the cord of his robe but wide-awake, opened the door. In a few words Elizabeth told him the same story she had told the soldiers.

"Father's not home, but I'll be ready in a minute. You wait in the office while I put some clothes on."

Elizabeth went into the office with Feldwebel Geissler at her heels and sat on the edge of Erik's desk. Almost immediately Erik was back and she watched him pack his stethoscope and drugs into his medical bag. He would also need a splint and thread and a needle to sew up the wound, she realized. She glanced over her shoulder. She could not whisper to Erik, for Feldwebel Geissler was right behind her.

"You'dbetteralsotakeasplintandyoumayhavetosewup awound," she spoke very fast, knitting her words together and hoping the *Feldwebel*'s knowledge of Dutch was scanty.

"What do you mean?" Erik had just closed his bag.

"He fell." Elizabeth blinked hard at Erik.

"He fell?"

"From his bed," Elizabeth improvised. "You know his bed is sky high." Elizabeth emphasized the word "sky." "It was a very long fall." She spoke the last three words slowly. Erik eyed her sharply and Elizabeth blinked harder.

"I'm glad you told me." Erik opened the bag again and put the necessary things in. "I'm ready."

Feldwebel Geissler had made up his mind to drive Erik and Elizabeth back to Swaenenburgh and he would not tolerate an argument. They would lose too much time at the roadblocks, and the sooner the doctor was with the patient, the better.

The trip back went fast. They zoomed by the barricades and the truck took the paved road that led to the front entrance of Swaenenburgh with breakneck speed. Erik's arm was around Elizabeth and now and then he gave her a little squeeze. For the first time in many months she felt close to him again. Through all their recent arguments and disagreements she had forgotten how fond she had always been of him. She had even forgotten how nice he smelled, of disinfectant and tobacco. Within the crook of his arm she moved closer to him.

The courtyard of Swaenenburgh was as busy as if it were noon instead of five o'clock in the morning. Major Schmidt had just returned with a small contingent of soldiers, but was urging them to make ready to leave again. The men, tired and disheveled, were gulping hot coffee and eating sandwiches as fast as they could. Major Schmidt appeared as fresh as if he had just got up from a long night's sleep, but his muddy boots and trousers showed that he had tramped through the fields and swamps all night. His sharp eyes did not miss a thing. He had seen the truck cross the drawbridge and he was waiting for it as it approached. He ignored Elizabeth and Erik as they clambered out of the vehicle, and addressed Feldwebel Geissler.

"You left the post I assigned to you," he snapped.

88

Feldwebel Geissler jumped to attention. "I, I thought—" he began.

"You left your post," Major Schmidt repeated. "I had given every soldier orders under no circumstance to leave his post."

"Herr Major, you must understand. Freule Elizabeth told me her father was seriously ill. She had to get a doctor fast. I thought in a matter of life and death I could help her. I didn't leave the post unattended; there were still twelve other soldiers there." Feldwebel Geissler pleaded in a frightened voice as if he were a small boy about to burst into tears instead of a big man, towering over his superior.

"The trouble with you, Geissler, is that you think too much," Major Schmidt said with cutting sarcasm. "You don't have to think. Just do as I tell you. Get back to your post," he barked. "I'll deal with you later." Major Schmidt turned his back on the *Feldwebel* and faced Elizabeth and Erik. Feldwebel Geissler scuffled away. Elizabeth saw him climb into his truck. It was indecent of Major Schmidt to treat him this way; Elizabeth was indignant, but she forgot all about Feldwebel Geissler when Major Schmidt addressed her.

"Is your father's sickness serious enough to warrant a trip to the doctor in the middle of the night?" Major Schmidt was obviously annoyed by the interruption Elizabeth had caused.

"Y-yes, he's v-very s-sick," Elizabeth stammered. She felt sick herself, sick with fear that Major Schmidt would not trust her and would go and look for himself.

"I told Freule van Swaenenburgh to immediately notify me in case there was a change in the Baron van Swaenenburgh's condition." Erik spoke with authority and his professional air seemed to satisfy Major Schmidt, for he became more friendly.

"I hope your father will recover soon, Freule Elizabeth," he said pleasantly. "Good-bye, Freule. Good-bye, Doctor."

"I'll never understand him." Elizabeth shuddered. "He's a terrible man."

"He likes to see people squirm," Erik said. "He had a lot of fun tonight with Geissler and us."

Jacob was waiting for them in the kitchen. "Well, you took your time getting back," he greeted Elizabeth. The anger in his voice made her realize how worried about her he had been. When she had been small and had hurt herself, he had always been furious with her, and the more she was hurt, the angrier he had been. Jacob took Erik by the arm and the two men went downstairs together.

Elizabeth remained in the kitchen so that she could warn Erik and Jacob if necessary. Sitting in Jacob's big chair, she watched the courtyard. Cars drove back and forth across the drawbridge and soldiers kept coming and going. She could hear Major Schmidt's voice shout commands, but no sound came from the dungeon. Elizabeth glanced at the clock. It was just half past five. Time would go faster if she kept busy. She would make breakfast. They all could do with some food after this night. She set the table in Jacob's office with an extra plate for Erik and she laid out her father's tray. She wondered if the Englishman would take any food. Maybe just a cup of tea? She took a cup and spoon from the cupboard and rinsed them out in the sink. But she had better not keep the cup on the table. If Major Schmidt walked in and found one cup unaccounted for, he might wonder. Elizabeth put the cup and spoon back. For that matter her father, who was supposedly gravely ill, would not eat his usual breakfast. Elizabeth cleared Nicolaas' tray and looked again at the clock. It was a few minutes past six. The time went slowly. She would see if her father was up and make him an early cup of tea. Elizabeth put the kettle over a low flame and tiptoed upstairs.

She heard Nicolaas' deep snoring as soon as she reached the first landing. Although she was tempted to walk into his room and wake him, she did not dare to. Jacob was very strict that nobody disturb Nicolaas. She hoped he would wake up soon. She would tell him everything that had happened during the night. Maybe he would finally shake off his apathy and respond to what was happening around him. Elizabeth settled herself on the landing. Here she could still watch the courtyard. A low, round window, from which the old Van Swaenenburghs had shot their cannons to protect the castle, gave a splendid view of the courtyard and the woods and fields in the distance. She saw Major Schmidt direct the last group of soldiers into a truck and climb into the seat next to the driver. Her eyes followed the truck as it went over the drawbridge and down the road. For the time being Major Schmidt was gone. Elizabeth opened the window and stuck her head out. The courtyard was peaceful and empty except for some birds pecking at crumbs. The morning smelled fresh. The bells of the monastery down in the village began to ring, calling the monks to early mass.

Father André! Elizabeth thought suddenly. That's where they would take the wounded man. That's where all the others had gone, those her father and Jacob had hidden. And this one would go tonight. She could not bear to have him in the house any longer than was necessary. How a wounded man, who was unable to walk, would get to the monastery Elizabeth did not know, but she was sure Erik would find a way. Jennie had often told her how Erik had whisked away prisoners under the very eyes of their German guards. Elizabeth went back to the kitchen to wait for Erik and Jacob.

"He'll be all right," were Jacob's first words when he and Erik emerged from the cellar. "Erik did a wonderful job," Jacob said. Erik only smiled. He seemed exhausted, but his smile more than Jacob's words assured Elizabeth that the Englishman would get well.

"Oh, Erik, you are wonderful." Elizabeth hugged Erik spontaneously. She thought of how young the Englishman had looked and she was glad that he was going to be all right.

"He's still a pretty sick man, though." Erik tempered her enthusiasm. "His shoulder wound is infected and his broken leg gives him much pain." Erik's face clouded momentarily. "I had to hurt him a lot. He was carrying on so that Jacob had to hold him down while I set his leg and cleaned out the wound."

"Don't tell me about it." Elizabeth shuddered. The deep, dark dungeon from which no sound had escaped throughout the man's two-hour ordeal was not a pleasant thought.

"Sit down for breakfast," she ordered. "You both deserve a good meal." She busied herself pouring tea and slicing bread before she sat down with them. "I'm glad he's doing nicely," she said casually between bites. "It'll make it easier to move him out of the dungeon tonight."

"Tonight?" A quick glance passed between Erik and Jacob, but Elizabeth seemed not to notice.

"You have to get him down to Father André, Erik." Elizabeth poured more tea. She saw Erik was about to protest. "Don't tell me it can't be done," she said. "He has to go."

"I wasn't going to say that it couldn't be done." Erik put down his knife and fork. "But it is something I hesitate to undertake," he said thoughtfully. "You realize that he has to be carried. I'd need at least two men besides Jacob to help me."

"Jennie told me you've carried out much more daring schemes. I'm sure you can do this too." Although she was not the least bit hungry anymore, Elizabeth forced herself to eat another slice of bread.

"One only does daring deeds when there's no choice," Jacob protested. "The man is safe here. By moving him, his life is endangered and so are the lives of any others who are involved. To move him now is lunacy," Jacob said tersely.

These were the same old arguments, Elizabeth thought wearily. She was tired of hearing them. They would never agree.

"Tonight when it's dark, he's going." Elizabeth pushed her chair back from the table. "You decide the best way to do it. I'm going to school."

"To school?" Jacob and Erik chorused in surprise.

"You should go to sleep," Erik said. "You were up half the night."

"Maybe a good nap will put some sense into your head." Jacob got up and began to prepare Nicolaas' breakfast. Elizabeth was exhausted and she felt the beginning of a dull headache, but under no circumstance would she stay home. Jacob and Erik would pester her all day. They would leave her no peace. At school the time would go fast. It would be five o'clock before she came home and that would leave only a few hours till dark. Elizabeth did not want to think of the next few hours, but she had complete faith in Erik. She was infuriated by his stubborn refusal to see her point of view, but she knew he was clever and resourceful. Major Schmidt would never catch Erik, she was sure. And tomorrow she would once more be safe, completely safe.

"I could not sleep a wink as long as he's in the house." Elizabeth stuffed her books into her bag.

"I don't understand how you can live with yourself," Erik burst out. "As long as you're safe, nothing matters to you. You think only of yourself. Don't you care what happens to other people?" He didn't get an answer to his question, for Elizabeth had left, slamming the kitchen door closed between them.

Chapter Six

How DIFFERENT IT WAS to ride through the woods in the daytime, Elizabeth thought. After yesterday's rain the earth smelled fresh and the branches of the trees, with the sunlight shining through the yellow leaves, formed a golden arch above her head. Elizabeth closed her eyes for a moment and lifted her face. The soft breeze blew on her skin. She took a deep breath and filled her lungs with the scent of birch and pine, and slowly the heavy, dull ache in her head eased. No matter how bad thing were, the woods always made her feel better, Elizabeth thought gratefully. She ducked to avoid a spider web that hung silver and shimmering in geometric perfection from a low branch.

She forced herself to think calmly about the day ahead. She would get through school as well as she could. After school, rather than depend on Erik's and Jacob's grudging help, she herself would go to Father André and arrange for the Englishman's move to the monastery.

She had been deep in thought, and before she knew it, she had come to the end of the woods. The road-block was still up at the signpost, and although she felt the same sinking fear she experienced whenever she came upon a German sentry, she approached the soldier outwardly calm. This time no questions were asked and the mere formality of showing her identity card got her through.

Elizabeth realized that all the talk at breakfast had made her late and she wasn't surprised when she didn't find Jennie waiting for her at their usual spot. Although Jennie usually waited, she probably had thought that Elizabeth had stayed home, because her father had taken a turn for the worse. As far as Jennie knew, Elizabeth had come in the middle of the night to get help for her father. She rode the remaining miles to school as fast as she could and slipped through the door just as the second bell rang.

In school Elizabeth was sleepy at first, but gradually

she became wide-awake and tense. She kept wondering what Jacob and Erik were doing and most of all what Major Schmidt was plotting. She couldn't wait to get to Father André. The moment the last bell had rung she was out of her seat, ignoring Jennie who, behind the teacher's back, was motioning her to wait.

With the wind blowing at her back, pushing her on, it did not take Elizabeth long to reach the village of Swaenenburgh. There was no sign of a roadblock anywhere and the main street was deserted. It was too early for the children to be out of school and the men were still working in the fields. In front of the Timmermans' house were Erik's motorbike, Dr. Timmermans' Renault and a row of baby carriages. From an open window of the office came the loud wail of an infant. Elizabeth turned off the main street into the poplar-lined, narrow lane that led to the monastery and the church.

They had been built by the same Frank van Swaenenburgh who had built the castle, and in the same simple medieval style. Both housed precious art treasures, carved statues, religious paintings of the Flemish school and the famed stained-glass windows. Like the castle, the monastery and church were safeguarded by a moat and a high stone wall against warfare and the robber gangs that roamed the land in those long-ago days. The moat had long since been filled in, but the wall was strong and unbroken. To its century-old bricks clung ivy and roses, and on the southern end it shielded the gardens from the wind. In the gardens, up against the sunny wall, Brother Sebastiaan, the head gardener, grew flowers that would grow nowhere else in the country.

Elizabeth pulled the big bell, a young monk opened the heavy door, and she followed him through the long corridor to Father André's study.

"Father André will be with you," the monk said and Elizabeth heard his sandals tap away over the stone floor.

Father André's study was as starkly simple as any other monk's cell, in accordance with the Franciscan vow of poverty. The walls were bare except for a crucifix and a portrait of Frank van Swaenenburgh that hung over Father André's desk. It was different from the portrait at Swaenenburgh and her ancestor wore monk's robes, but it had always made Elizabeth feel at home in Father André's study.

"Elizabeth, I am so glad to see you." Father André was standing in the doorway. He was an old man and even the heavy brown robes he wore could not hide the frailty of his body. "I expected you," he said in his soft voice. "I saw Erik this morning. Sit down, please."

Elizabeth felt anger rise inside her. Erik had run to

99

Father André as soon as he had had a chance and now Father André was against her too.

"I hope you will also listen to me." Elizabeth was on the verge of bursting out in anger against Erik and Father André himself, but she held back her temper. In spite of his frail, old looks, there was something formidable about Father André that made you mind the words you spoke to him. Even her father and Jacob curbed their language in his presence.

"Erik never listens to me and he never wants to do what I want him to do," Elizabeth said. "He doesn't care what happens to us and to Swaenenburgh."

"You are wrong, Elizabeth," Father André said. "Erik came to me this morning to arrange for the Englishman to be taken here tonight."

"He did?" Elizabeth had braced herself for a long and tiresome debate with Father André, but now there seemed nothing to argue about. She felt limp and tired.

"Erik has taken care of everything," Father André said.

"I'm sorry," Elizabeth mumbled awkwardly. She stood up. "Then there's really nothing for me to talk with you about."

"Don't go yet." Father André's veined, transparent hand motioned toward the chair. "There's something very important I want to talk with you about." He waited till she sat down again.

"It's not a pleasant thought." Father André rearranged some books on his desk. "But we have to count on the possibility that things may go wrong." He paused to let his words sink in. "If that happens, I'm most concerned about you, Elizabeth."

"You mean Major Schmidt will find out that the Englishman was hidden at Swaenenburgh." Elizabeth spoke with difficulty. Her mouth had gone dry. It was a possibility she had refused to consider.

But that was not what Father André had in mind. In his precise, scholarly way, as if he were teaching catechism, he explained to Elizabeth exactly how the Englishman would be transported to the monastery. Erik and three brothers would carry him on a stretcher, while two other brothers led the way. Erik had taken every precaution that Major Schmidt could not link the Englishman with Swaenenburgh. The man had been hardly conscious when she and Jacob had been with him. Erik was sure he would not remember them. Today he had seen no one but Erik. They would drug him before they carried him out. The chance that they would be caught leaving the house and going into the woods was slight. Jacob knew the exact times the sentries came around and he had helped Erik plan the trip to the last detail. Every second was accounted for. The greatest hazard was getting through the woods and the fields. If they were caught at that point, however, Elizabeth was safe. Erik and the brothers had their story ready. They would say that they had kept the man hidden in the abandoned forester's house in the woods. Erik knew that it had not been searched and he had gone over in the morning to make it look as if somebody had recently been there.

"I am sure that you will go free," Father André assured Elizabeth. "Nothing will make Erik or my brothers talk."

"I know they won't." Elizabeth felt miserably ashamed for having been angry with Erik, who had taken such endless, painstaking care to protect her and her family.

"If something goes wrong, however, you will suffer most, Elizabeth," Father André said solemnly. "For the rest of your life you will have to carry the burden of the knowledge that this was your doing. You have to live with your own conscience, Elizabeth. I want you to be very sure that this is really what you want."

She should have known, Elizabeth thought. Father André did not agree with her at all. She would have liked to argue with him the way she argued with Jacob and Erik. She would like to tell him that she didn't want anything to happen to Erik or the brothers or the unknown Englishman. She only wanted not to be hurt herself. She wanted only to be safe. But how could she talk about being safe with Father André, who lived in danger every minute of his life?

"I don't want you to answer me now." Father André rose from his chair, to indicate to Elizabeth that her visit had come to an end. "Just think about it." His handshake was warm and firm for such an old, frail man. "Don't forget to go see Brother Sebastiaan," he reminded her. "He would never forgive me if you didn't pay him a visit too."

Elizabeth found Brother Sebastiaan weeding the garden. Sixty years of tending flowers had bent Brother Sebastiaan's back and every time Elizabeth saw him he had grown a little closer to the earth. He always reminded her of a gnome with magic powers. Under his hands, now gnarled and twisted by old age, his garden grew more dazzlingly beautiful than any other garden she had ever seen. The gardens of the monastery were Brother Sebastiaan's single passion in life and he could not bear to be away from them. He left them only to hear mass and nobody knew when he ate or when he slept.

"I hope the gardens in paradise are as beautiful as mine," Brother Sebastiaan often said. "Otherwise I do not much care for going there."

As soon as he saw Elizabeth come down the path, Brother Sebastiaan stopped weeding and came hobbling toward her, his arms outstretched.

"Elizabeth, you haven't come to see me in a long time." Brother Sebastiaan reproached her. "I have missed you. You haven't even seen my new rose." He pulled her impatiently back along the path.

"Look." Brother Sebastiaan cut a rose for her. "See what perfection of petals." He showed her his other flowers. There was always so much to see, she could spend hours here, but she must go. Elizabeth said good-bye and when she had reached the door in the wall, she turned to enjoy for another moment the perfect beauty of Brother Sebastiaan's garden. The tiny monk was weeding his flower bed again, his dusty brown robe blending completely with the earth and the leaves.

She cycled home slowly and all the way she kept thinking about Father André's words. She argued with herself. Should she let the Englishman stay or should she send him away? She didn't know what to do any-more and she was nowhere near a decision when she reached Swaenenburgh. Erik's motorbike was up against the kitchen wall. Elizabeth didn't want to meet him before she had made up her mind about the Eng-lishman. She crossed the courtyard to walk for a while around the moat.

On the grassy bank, almost on the spot where Kurt had been sitting a few months ago, sat Feldwebel Geissler.

"Freule Elizabeth." Feldwebel Geissler rose. Elizabeth noticed that he was wearing his long overcoat and cap. A bulging duffel bag lay beside him.

"You're leaving?" she asked.

"I'm going to the Russian front," Feldwebel Geissler answered. "I'm waiting for the truck to pick me up. I was just taking some last pictures." He pointed to a small camera on top of his luggage. "I'll send them to my daughter. I always told her in my letters about the lovely castle I was living in."

"You're going to the Russian front because of what happened yesterday? Major Schmidt is sending you." Elizabeth felt shaken. Feldwebel Geissler was a German and until last night he had been only an enemy. But he had helped her and because of that he was sent away. Very few German soldiers ever returned from the eastern front. "I'm sorry," she said awkwardly.

"Nobody's sending me and don't be sorry for me. I want to go." Feldwebel Geissler looked out over the moat and the woods below. "I'm a soldier, Freule Elizabeth," he said. "But what we're doing in your country is not worthy of a good soldier. It's maybe good enough for Major Schmidt." He shrugged. "Everybody has to live with his own conscience. But it's not good enough for Feldwebel Geissler. I want my daughter to be proud of me. Would you . . ." He hesitated for a moment. "Would you, please, take a picture of me for my daughter?"

Feldwebel Geissler stood very straight with his chest out and his hand at his head in salute as Elizabeth pressed the button.

When Elizabeth walked into the house, there was nobody in the kitchen. Maybe Erik and Jacob were with the patient. She opened the cellar door, took one of the flashlights off the peg, and went down the stairs. In the cellar she slid the panel aside and went on down the spiral staircase. At the last turn she saw that a small light was burning in the dungeon.

A candle was on the table and a cot was pulled up next to it. The rest of the room was in darkness. There was nobody in the dungeon except for the huddled shape on the cot, covered with blankets. Elizabeth came closer. The man opened his eyes.

"A little water," he whispered. "I'm so thirsty."

There was a glass of water on the table and a small basin with a washcloth and towel. Elizabeth had to support his head while he drank. His skin was hot and dry. She took the cloth and bathed his face.

"That feels good." The man fell back against the pillows and closed his eyes. Elizabeth watched him.

"One has to live with his own conscience" and "You have to live with your own conscience, Elizabeth." Two very different people had said exactly the same thing. Elizabeth knew that she would never forgive herself if something happened to the Englishman and Erik and the brothers. As long as the Englishman was in the house, she would be afraid. But there were worse things than being afraid. She tucked the blanket carefully around the man's wounded shoulder.

"And what do you think you're doing here?" Elizabeth had not heard Erik come down the stairs. "Nobody is allowed here but me." Erik was fuming.

"I gave him some water and I washed his face. I hope that was all right." Elizabeth's casual answer only made Erik angrier.

"For God's sake, Elizabeth. You drive me crazy." Erik pushed his hand through his thick hair. "I'm trying my best to make things as safe for you as possible and you come and show your face to him. Get upstairs, immediately."

"After I have straightened his bed." Elizabeth smoothed the top sheet. "Making beds is Jacob's weak point. Until he's well enough to do it himself, I'll make his bed for him."

Chapter Seven

Elizabeth knew that if she had to choose again between hiding the Englishman in the dungeon or leaving him to be found by Major Schmidt, she would choose no differently. Yet during the next five weeks she often deplored her decision.

The Englishman's name was David Greene and during the first days of his stay he was very sick and needed much care. With Nicolaas still bedridden it was impossible for Jacob alone to care for the two patients. Elizabeth had to stay home from school.

The problem of caring for David was complicated by

the danger his presence caused all of them. Elizabeth and Jacob had worked out a careful system so that they should not be caught unaware. One of them kept watch in the kitchen while the other was with David. Elizabeth didn't know which she feared more, to be upstairs and perhaps have to deal with a visit from Major Schmidt or one of his soldiers or to be in the dungeon and not know what was waiting for her upstairs. It was agreed that if one of the Germans should come, the person in the kitchen would talk loudly to warn the one who was coming up. It was by no means a foolproof arrangement, Elizabeth realized, but it was the best they could think of.

Her uneasiness about their safety and her hurry to get back upstairs as soon as possible often made her gruff with David. She knew, of course, that none of what had happened was his fault, yet she couldn't help feeling that he was the cause of all her troubles, and the sooner he was gone, the better. When she made his bed in the morning, pulling the sheets and blankets tight so that he would lie comfortably, she ordered him crisply to turn on his left side, onto his back and on his right side. David amiably did whatever she told him to do. Her curtness did not bother him at all. After the long, lonesome night he was eager for company and he liked to talk to Elizabeth while she made his bed and straightened the room. His favorite topic was how miraculously lucky he had been to get to Swaenenburgh. He told her over and over again how he had crawled on hands and knees away from the burning plane and his dead friend. He had covered miles of fields and woods. Every time he had come near a house he had thought of asking for help, but at the last moment he had always turned away, afraid that the people would turn him over to the German authorities. At last he had come to Swaenenburgh.

"In the moonlight it looked to me like a fairy-tale castle," he said once. "And it is, complete with a fairy-tale princess. Are you listening to me, Elizabeth?"

"Yes, I am. Stretch out on your back now." Elizabeth plumped the pillows and tucked the top sheet in. She had not really paid attention to David's story. She had learned very quickly to listen with only one ear, while her other ear listened for Jacob's knock on the door.

"For a brave girl you're remarkably beautiful and feminine, Elizabeth." David watched her, leaning back comfortably in the pillows. "Before I met you, I thought all girls in the Dutch underground were big, strapping females, who pushed drunken German soldiers into the canal." He burst out laughing at Elizabeth's horrified expression.

"Hush, don't make so much noise." David's hearty laugh, now that he was getting better, was one more worry to Elizabeth. "I'm not a member of the underground and I'm not at all brave," she said, but secretly she was pleased. Nobody had ever told her she was beautiful. Eva was the undisputed beauty of the family.

But brave! It upset her to think of anyone saying that, and to hide her embarrassment, she straightened an imaginary fold in the top sheet.

"You are brave and beautiful," David insisted. "When I'm back home, I will sometimes close my eyes and I'll see you just as you are now. After the war is over, you must come visit my wife and me. I'll show you Oxford and Cambridge and our small village in Sussex." Although Elizabeth was in a hurry to get back to the safety of the kitchen, she couldn't leave David, not right now when he wanted so much to tell her about his wife and his home. She let him talk, and while he talked, she caught a glimpse of the fear that he kept so carefully hidden from everybody, that he would never see his wife and his home again.

After a week Elizabeth went back to school. David had improved enough so that he could be left alone for most of the day. Even Nicolaas was making progress. Although he still couldn't talk, he had understood everything he had been told about David, and he showed avid interest in Jacob's faithful reports about what was happening in the dungeon.

"It does Mijnheer Nicolaas a world of good to have

111

somebody in the dungeon again. I told you so," Jacob said to Elizabeth. "He's less apathetic and shows interest in his surroundings again. What do you plan to do after David is gone?"

Although Elizabeth had also noticed her father's improved spirits, she refused to credit the change in him to David's presence.

"Get a good night's sleep," she answered. She thought with yearning of the nights she would sleep again without interruption till late in the morning. Now she woke several times during the night and lay awake for hours, listening for any sound in the house that might mean danger. It was amazing how many noises there were she could not explain. Doors kept banging and the stairs squeaked even when nobody walked on them. Twice she had run downstairs, sure that Major Schmidt was knocking on the kitchen door, only to find that a shutter was loose and banging against the outside wall. She spent hours, shivering in her bathrobe, at the top of the stairs and went back to bed only when she heard Jacob get up and go into the kitchen.

Sometimes she had the feeling that she was living in a beleaguered fortress and she could barely wait for the moment she could leave for school. But once in school she couldn't wait to get home again, to see with her own eyes that everything was the same as she had left it that morning. During classes she thought of all the things that could possibly go wrong and then one afternoon she had suddenly been overwhelmed by the certainty that something had gone wrong.

She went to the teacher and, pretending she wasn't feeling good, asked to be excused early. She rode her bicycle as fast as she could and arrived breathless at Swaenenburgh, where she found Jacob in the kitchen, sipping his afternoon tea.

Elizabeth didn't know what she had expected, but certainly not to find him sitting quietly with his pipe and his newspaper. She tried to pull herself together, but she couldn't quite steady her voice.

"H-how are Father and David?"

"Mijnheer Nicolaas and David are still napping." Jacob poured Elizabeth a cup of tea too. "You're getting out early these days," he remarked.

"One of the teachers is sick," Elizabeth lied. Although she was thirsty, she didn't dare drink her tea for fear her hand would tremble as she held the cup. She still felt shaky.

"Even so, you must have ridden as if the devil were right behind you." Jacob examined his watch. "It isn't even three yet. What did you expect to find?" he asked, puffing on his pipe.

"Major Schmidt, I guess." Elizabeth laughed lamely. It was no use trying to fool Jacob. "I'm scared, Jacob," she confessed. "I can't help thinking that one day he'll realize. He'll remember. In all his search for the missing pilot the only place he skipped was Swaenenburgh."

Major Schmidt and his soldiers still hadn't given up. They had searched every house in the village and the surrounding area and sometimes in the middle of the night his soldiers would suddenly appear and search a house all over again. The farms in the neighborhood of the spot where the plane had crashed were periodically raided and Major Schmidt himself had paid a visit to the monastery, something he had never done before.

"Even if he searches Swaenenburgh, he still won't find David." Jacob stuffed his pipe with his homegrown tobacco, and blew a puff of foul-smelling smoke into the room. "Nobody can find the dungeon, unless you know where it is and he doesn't. Anyhow, he won't search."

"Why not?"

"Because he's a fool," Jacob said. "He understands nothing about people. Why do you think he hardly bothers the monks?" Jacob didn't even wait for an answer. "It's because he thinks Father André is a weak old man, who can't do anything but lie on his knees and pray. He doesn't think much of you either." Jacob's eyes rested on Elizabeth and she read in them the same pride and affection he had always shown when, as a little girl, she had done something especially bright and clever.

"He doesn't know that you are a real Van Swaenenburgh."

If Jacob meant by a real Van Swaenenburgh somebody who was bold and fearless in the face of danger, Elizabeth did not feel at all like a Van Swaenenburgh when she was playing chess with Major Schmidt. It unnerved her completely to sit opposite him, with the chessboard between them, and feel his eyes upon her all the time to see how she would move. He conversed courteously and accepted graciously his loss of a game, but it froze Elizabeth's blood to think of the two of them, pushing kings and queens around while all the time they were sitting right on top of the major's elusive quarry.

Every night at ten o'clock Major Schmidt went down to the village for a beer and came home promptly at the stroke of midnight. Thursday was no exception. These two hours were the only time in which Elizabeth could be reasonably sure nothing could happen. At supper Thursdays, with the dreaded game hanging over her head, she was never hungry and she had made it a habit to drink a cup of coffee and eat a sandwich with David after she had left Major Schmidt. But always she kept her eyes on the clock on the dungeon table and a few minutes before the stroke of twelve she ran, no matter what she interrupted.

"Stay a little longer," David always begged, but Elizabeth could not be shaken. Not a second longer would she stay in the dungeon.

"You're like Cinderella," he teased her as she ran upstairs. Elizabeth bolted the door to the dungeon and slid the panel back with the utmost care. She checked that no crack was showing. What could have happened to Cinderella was nothing compared to what could happen to all of them, if she were not careful.

After six weeks Erik judged David well enough to leave. His shoulder wound had healed and the cast had been off his leg more than a week. On Jacob's arm David had practiced walking and now he walked well by himself. Every day he covered a few miles, going industriously up and down the long end of the dungeon. Elizabeth had taught him enough Dutch to get by a German guard. He was as ready as he would ever be.

Erik had arranged for his departure. He would be picked up by a British plane at an appointed spot, some ninety miles away. One of Father André's brothers would accompany him on the train. David would travel disguised as a monk with falsified identity papers and he would be met by a courier at the station of his destination. The courier would take him on foot and by night the last of the way. The idea of the train trip filled

David with dread, but it had to be done that way. Since his escape the area around Swaenenburgh was much too closely guarded for an English plane to land unobserved.

On a Saturday morning in the middle of October Father André arrived at Swaenenburgh, wearing two sets of monk's robes. When Elizabeth came back from school a little after twelve, she found them all in the dungeon: Erik, Jacob, and Father André with a monk. For a moment Elizabeth looked around, wondering where David had gone.

"Let me introduce you to Brother Albertus." Father André's eyes twinkled. Elizabeth hardly recognized David as the big monk with the tonsured head.

"They have to go," Erik urged. "Under no circumstance can David miss his train." Behind one another they climbed the narrow steps to the cellar. Elizabeth and David came last. At the first bend in the stairs David turned. A candle was still burning on the table. His bed was unmade and his book was lying facedown on the page where he had stopped reading that morning.

"Strange—how safe it looks." David spoke softly. "So safe that I wish I were right back in my bed."

"You'll be all right." Elizabeth took his hand and squeezed it hard.

In the kitchen David stood blinking. He had been in

the dark a long time and had to get used again to the daylight. It was strange to see him in the everyday surroundings of the kitchen, Elizabeth thought. She had never realized how tall he was. His robe was too short for his long legs and his bare ankles and feet looked naked and cold in the rough sandals. Elizabeth remembered the many times she had tucked the blankets around those feet.

"We must leave now, David," Father André urged. The men shook hands quickly without speaking. There was nothing to say anymore. Then David bent down to Elizabeth. There was a very special tenderness in his eyes.

"Good-bye, Cinderella. Don't forget, we'll see each other in England," he said and kissed her.

Erik and Elizabeth watched the two brown monks as they crossed the drawbridge and Elizabeth was filled with relief when the last glimpse of David's brown habit disappeared behind the trees. Father André and his brothers were a familiar sight in the woods and in and around the village. The German guards seldom checked them. David was still quite safe. The real danger, she knew, would start when he got on the train.

The rest of the afternoon Elizabeth helped Jacob empty out the dungeon. They stripped the cot and Elizabeth washed the sheets and blankets. Jacob took the books and puzzles that David had used back to the library and the dungeon was again what it had always been, a dark black hole in the ground.

"It's empty without David," Jacob remarked.

"It's nice and neat," Elizabeth said. "I'm hungry after all this work. Let's eat." But neither she nor Jacob ate much.

"They're on the train now," Jacob said when they were halfway through their meal. He repeated that same phrase with small variations all through the evening.

"They must have got off the train." Jacob stirred his tea. "I hope they had no trouble contacting the courier."

Later in the evening Jacob turned off the lights and opened the curtains. It was a dark, moonless night with only a few stars out.

"A good night for walking," he remarked. "This is one night when one doesn't need a moon."

At twelve o'clock Jacob went upstairs to look in on Nicolaas, before going to sleep himself.

"You'd better go to sleep too, Elizabeth," Jacob said. "If everything has gone according to plan, the plane has taken off."

The first night without David. The night she had looked forward to for six long weeks. Elizabeth tossed around on her bed, unable to fall asleep. She heard Major Schmidt's car come thundering over the draw-bridge and after a few hours she heard him leave again. If she could only be sure that David had got away. It was still dark when Elizabeth finally gave up trying to fall asleep. One more sleepless night would do her no harm, she told herself. In the morning she would have news of David. She had an appointment with Father André at one o'clock and she would hear then how everything had gone. And after today she could sleep all she wanted.

Elizabeth watched the daylight seep into her room, and when she heard the bells of the monastery chime for the early six o'clock mass, she got up and dressed. She sat down at her desk, hoping to finish her homework before breakfast. But the story she had to paraphrase for French was silly and she didn't care at all who had won the War of the Roses. She closed her books.

After breakfast she spent the rest of the morning with Nicolaas. He was fidgety and restless, and although he could not tell her, Elizabeth knew that he too was worried about David. At eleven she couldn't wait any longer. She told Jacob that she would go to the Timmermans' and he was eager for her to leave. Maybe Erik had news.

At the Timmermans' Erik was busy with a patient in the office and Jennie wasn't home. Elizabeth waited with Mrs. Timmermans in the living room.

"We haven't heard anything yet," Mrs. Timmermans

told her. Elizabeth drank one cup of sugarless ersatz coffee and manfully swallowed a piece of Mrs. Timmermans' cake.

"Do take another piece. It's good for you. You're much too thin," Mrs. Timmermans insisted. She was a bad but enthusiastic cook and was always trying the latest recipes. The lack of proper ingredients every housewife suffered from nowadays didn't stop her. This cake was made with beet sugar and minced tulip bulbs. Elizabeth was glad when Erik came and she could gracefully refuse a third piece.

Elizabeth left her bike at Erik's house and rode on the back of his motorcycle to the monastery. When they got there, it was still too early.

"Let's wait in the garden," Elizabeth said. She felt cold and shivery. "It'll be much warmer and sunnier there than inside. I'll ask Brother Sebastiaan to show you his new rose. He's awfully proud of it." Without waiting for Erik's answer, she walked along the wall and opened the small side door that led into the garden.

As always Elizabeth was caught afresh by the beauty of the garden. Brother Sebastiaan's roses were still in full bloom against the south wall and the chrysanthemums were at their peak. The grass around the old apple tree was purple with meadow saffron and red and orange berries decorated the leafless bushes. But there was no sign of Brother Sebastiaan.

121

"That's the first time I've come here and he didn't meet me." Elizabeth walked along the path, careful not to step on a leaf or flower. "Maybe he's in the shed." She rattled the doorknob. "It's locked. I don't understand."

"He must be in the refectory, eating lunch," Erik said.

"Brother Sebastiaan never eats lunch in the refectory. He must be here. He's always in the garden." Elizabeth scanned the flower beds, sure that she would soon see a small brown shape weeding among the colorful flowers.

"There's Father André!" Erik exclaimed. He had seen the priest enter the garden from the monastery. Elizabeth forgot about Brother Sebastiaan as she hurried after Erik.

"Do you have news?" Erik asked as soon as they had reached the priest.

"Did David get away?" It was all Elizabeth could think about.

"The plane left on time. I just got word. David is probably home with his wife by now." But there was little joy in Father André's voice.

"Is something wrong, Father?" Erik took the old priest's arm and led him to a bench. They sat down beside him.

"I hoped you hadn't come yet." Father André's voice trembled slightly. "I came here, because I wanted to be alone in the garden for a while before I spoke to anybody."

"Do you want us to leave?" Elizabeth was worried. She had never seen Father André so old and frail.

"No, no." Father André put his thin hand over Elizabeth's. "You may as well know right away. Somebody betrayed the courier to the Germans. He was arrested and taken from his home this morning."

"And the brother?" Erik asked.

"They made the courier talk. Our brother was arrested too, just as he was about to board the train," Father André said. "He is dead.".

"Oh, no," Elizabeth cried. "Who was it?" Through her mind flashed the faces of all the young and able-bodied monks of the monastery. "What did they do to him?" she cried.

"They didn't do anything to him," Father André said. "He died of a heart attack in his cell at the police station. It was a merciful death, Elizabeth. He did not suffer."

"A heart attack?" Elizabeth asked indignantly. "That's impossible. They must have done something. How would a young man die of a heart attack?"

"He wasn't young. He was a very old man." Father André stood up and turned his back toward them and touched Brother Sebastiaan's new roses.

"Tell me who it was. Please, Father André," Elizabeth said, but Father André remained silent. Erik sat with his head bent and didn't speak either. "Please, tell me," Elizabeth insisted.

"Father André and I arranged for Brother Sebastiaan to go with David, Elizabeth," Erik said when Father André still didn't speak.

"Brother Sebastiaan is dead?" Elizabeth asked, hoping somebody would say no.

"Yes, Elizabeth," Father André said.

For a while Brother Sebastiaan's rare roses were nothing but a blurry pink blob before her eyes.

"Why did you send him?" Elizabeth wiped her eyes with the back of her hand. "He was too old for this kind of work. He should have died in his garden, not locked up in a police cell like a common criminal."

"He was my most trusted helper. He went many times," Father André said. He picked one of the roses and laid it in Elizabeth's lap. "You see, Elizabeth, he felt very strongly about what we are doing. He loved flowers and beauty and he thought that every man should be happy and free to enjoy God's beautiful world."

For a time the three sat on the bench without talking.

"We must go home, Elizabeth," Erik said. "Father André should rest." The priest was sitting with his hands between his knees and his head low in utter weariness.

"No, Erik, I cannot rest," Father André said. "I have so much to do." He lifted his head and smiled a little. "If Brother Sebastiaan were here, he would remind me that every man is like a gardener. And it is the lazy gardener who lays down his hoe and lets the weeds grow and thereby fails to save the flowers."

"Is there anything I can help you with?" Erik asked.

"Maybe," Father André said. "I have to find a temporary hiding place for a father and a daughter. They are Jews. Through unfortunate circumstances the people who promised me to hide them permanently can't have them till next month. I don't dare leave them in Amsterdam any longer," Father André explained. "The father can stay here in the monastery for the time being, but I don't know what to do about the daughter." He turned to Elizabeth. "I'm sure you remember her. They used to live in Swaenenburgh. Her name is Roza Cohen."

Roza! For one short moment Elizabeth hesitated. Tonight and the nights after were the ones she had been waiting for. She thought of her bed and the lovely empty dungeon. She twirled the rose between her fingers. Its petals were a deep, warm pink, arranged in graceful symmetry around a strong golden heart. Brother Sebastiaan had created many new roses in his lifetime, but this one, his last, was the most beautiful of all. Elizabeth picked it up and put it in the buttonhole of her coat.

"Roza will stay at Swaenenburgh for as long as she needs to," she said.

Chapter Eight

THE FOLLOWING WEDNESDAY Elizabeth took the train to Amsterdam to meet Roza and Mr. Cohen and bring them to Swaenenburgh. Sitting in the empty compartment of the train, Elizabeth wished she had been less brave and let somebody else come.

At first Erik had planned to go. He went every Wednesday to attend a medical clinic, but at the last moment Dr. Timmermans had got sick. It was impossible for Erik to leave and Elizabeth had volunteered to go instead.

"You don't have to go if you're afraid to," Erik had

told Elizabeth. "I can get one of the members of the underground to do it. Somebody ought to be there to keep an eye on them and take Roza to Swaenenburgh, but it doesn't have to be you." Elizabeth, however, had insisted.

"You told me the train trip would not be dangerous, at least not for me," she had reminded him. Erik had explained that all one had to do was stay near Roza and her father but under no circumstance make contact with them. If they were arrested on the way, Elizabeth was to go on as if nothing had happened, since there was not anything she could do all by herself. In Swaenenburgh she would report to Erik where and when the arrest had taken place. He would notify the underground and they would see what they could do. But because the Cohens had been given falsified papers, none of this was likely to occur.

"Even if we don't speak together, it'll make Roza feel good that I'm there and I know best how to get her safely to Swaenenburgh," Elizabeth said. "Nobody knows the back roads and woods as well as I do." To this Erik had to agree.

She had taken a book along for the trip, but after she read the same page four times and still didn't know what it was all about, she gave up and stuffed the book back into her handbag. She would have welcomed the opportunity to talk to somebody, but since she had left early, the train was empty. Elizabeth gazed out the window. Fall had come. The late harvest was in, the wheat and rye fields lay empty under the sunny sky, and in the cherry orchards the scarecrows, perched at the tops of trees, were the only reminder of the lost summer.

In Utrecht Elizabeth was to change trains. She checked the contents of her purse twice to be sure she had everything, and long before the train pulled into the station, she put on her coat and gloves. The trip from Utrecht to Amsterdam was short and swift since the train was an express, in contrast with the slow local from Swaenenburgh, and before Elizabeth knew it, she was in Amsterdam. She crossed the street and walked in the direction of the Royal Palace. She still had more than three hours before she was to meet Roza and Mr. Cohen, and the time would go faster if she spent it visiting some of her favorite spots.

Long ago, before the war, the times that Elizabeth had visited Amsterdam had been the highlights of the year. Nicolaas believed in taking his family places and showing them his beloved city. In the winter they'd go to the circus and the museums, and Elizabeth would sit next to her father, dressed in resplendent evening clothes, and listen to the Amsterdam Concertgebouw Orchestra and the Opera. In the summer they'd go on boat rides through the canals and to the zoo to see the baby animals. Although Elizabeth had been in Brussels, Berlin, Paris, Rome and other big cities, no city was as beautiful as Amsterdam.

It's changed a lot, Elizabeth thought. There were so many soldiers that the people of the city seemed lost among them. Even though it was sunny and warm for the time of the year, the sidewalk cafés were empty except for German soldiers and their girlfriends. Amsterdam had been a city of flowers and music, with jingling street organs, brass band parades, flower carts and barges full of flowers in the canals. Now the organs and flower carts had disappeared from the street corners and Elizabeth was struck by the silence and drabness of the streets.

The changed face of the city had not affected her so much a year ago, the last time she had been in Amsterdam. She had gone with Jennie to visit Roza and the three of them had walked all over town, because Roza with her yellow star could not ride in the trolley. Since she also was not allowed in the restaurants or the parks, they leaned over a bridge while they ate the picnic lunch Roza had brought. There was nothing today to prevent Elizabeth from taking the trolley or having a cup of coffee somewhere, but she preferred to walk.

Some things remained the same, though. When Elizabeth crossed the bridge, the blind violinist still fiddled his scratchy tune, and at the square in front of the palace, the Punch and Judy show still played. A few war-worn soldiers, probably on leave from the Russian front, stood by unsmiling, unable to understand the droll remarks of Punch and Judy. Elizabeth turned and walked back to the station. She would have some lunch in the restaurant on the first platform, where she was to meet the Cohens, and she'd wait there until they came.

There was a large crowd in front of the station, but Elizabeth did not pay attention. Her mind was wholly occupied with meeting Roza and Mr. Cohen and she was eager to study the layout. Erik had told her to take one of the tables in the restaurant where she could watch people come up the stairs. She still had to wait a little more than two hours, but she wanted to be sure to secure a seat in the right spot. She pushed the door open and went inside the station.

It was filled with people and a long line was waiting at one of the entrances to the trains. Never since the war had started had Elizabeth seen the station so busy. For a second it took her right back years ago, when she had traveled with her father and, holding onto his hand, had been afraid of getting lost among the gay, bustling holiday crowds. Then she realized that these were no gay holiday travelers.

They were mostly old men and women and mothers with small children. They carried suitcases and oddly shaped bundles. Some were obviously wealthy, others poor, but they all wore the yellow Star of David. They were Jews on their way to Westerbork, the deportation camp in the eastern part of the country.

And in between the people were the soldiers. Great, massive hulks of green-gray, armed with rifles with bayonets fixed. They wore helmets and their boots were polished to a shine as if they were on military parade and had to display their power to a mighty enemy. They towered over everybody else and shoved aside whoever happened to be in their way. Sometimes it was an old woman who, tottering under a heavy knapsack, could not see where she was going. Another time it was a child who, barely able to walk and seeking support, had clasped his short arms around a soldier's leg.

Elizabeth's first thought was of Roza and Mr. Cohen. She frantically scanned the faces around her. *Don't let me find them here,* she prayed silently. *Oh, dear God, don't let them be here.* The place was a nightmare and she would have liked to step right out of it, but she couldn't. She first had to make sure about Roza and Mr. Cohen.

An officer in charge had opened the gate to the trains and slowly but inescapably the line was put into motion. Soldiers, acting as guards, urged the people to move faster. Many of the old men and women wanted to look back for the last time, but even that most guards did not allow. If someone did not walk fast enough, he was pushed.

"*Schneller, schneller*," the guards shouted in unison till their command to walk faster became a chant, and pleased by its rhythm, they shouted louder and pushed harder.

Although Roza and Mr. Cohen were as familiar to Elizabeth as her own relatives, it was hard to recognize anyone. One face was like another, for the same emotions of fear and despair made everybody curiously alike. And some faces were altogether without identity. They were wiped clean of any expression. These people did not fear anymore or hope, but had resigned themselves, Elizabeth thought. Their neat, small pieces of luggage told her that they had been packed and ready for days, and to them their final departure came almost as a relief. What they had feared most had happened and now there was nothing to be afraid of anymore. They walked upright through the gate, they did not cry when they looked back for the last time, and their fearlessness infuriated the guards.

An old rabbi with a long white beard calmly murmured his prayers as he walked up to the gate. When he passed the guards, one of them pulled off his black hat and laughingly held it up for the other soldiers to see, shouting an obscenity.

"Say a prayer for me, old rabbi, and I'll give you back your pretty hat." The guard guffawed.

"May God forgive you and your people for the suffering you have brought upon the people of Israel." The rabbi's voice did not quaver and his serene old face did not change, not even when he saw the butt of the gun coming down on him.

Elizabeth had averted her eyes, unable to watch the guard pull the old man out of the line and hit him again and again till he finally lay motionless at the guard's feet. But there was no escape from horror. It was all around her.

The worst scenes took place in front of a table at the far end of the hall where four officials were stamping papers. A voice over the loudspeaker announced that time was running out and people were fighting to get to the officials and plead with them. They had brought certificates, hoping at the last moment to obtain a stamp that would at least reprieve them from this transport. A woman, who herself had been given the desired stamp, but whose husband had not, began to scream. She was carried away by two armed guards while the officials kept stamping papers as if nothing had happened.

Elizabeth would have liked to believe that one day, when the Germans had lost the war, all these people would come back, but she knew it wouldn't happen that way. For many the end of the war, if and when, would come too late. They were too old and too weak or too young and too frail to survive.

In her starless coat Elizabeth felt hideously conspicuous and guilty that among all these doomed people she was the only one who was free to leave. And when she was sure that Mr. Cohen and Roza were not among the crowd, she was glad that she didn't have to look for them anymore and that she could walk with her eyes down. Very slowly Elizabeth made her way toward the exit.

When she was almost at the door, a small boy, carrying a big, yellow teddy bear, tugged at her sleeve.

"Bear and I are going on the train," he told her proudly. "We were never allowed to go on the train, but today we may." His eyes were shining. "I hope I can sit at the window. Are you going too?"

Elizabeth, speechless, could only shake her head. She blindly pushed on. Somehow she reached the door, and when she showed her identity card, the guard let her through and she found herself miraculously on an outside platform.

The platform was empty, but across the tracks she could see the trains for Westerbork. People were piling in fast. They weren't passenger trains. They were closed cattle cars.

"I hope I can sit at the window." It was as if she felt

the boy's small hand, tugging at her sleeve. *I'll never forget it*, Elizabeth thought. *Even if I live to be a hundred years old, I'll still hear his voice.* She wished she could move, but she was afraid her legs would buckle under her if she took a step. She felt as if she had cried for days and had no tears left. Sitting on an empty luggage cart, she watched dry-eyed as the guards pushed one after another into the waiting trains. They were in such a hurry that they did not allow anybody to pick up a package that had been dropped, or reach out for a small hand that had been let go in the scuffle. The people were swallowed up by the dark insides of the trains as if they were insatiable monsters whose appetites for human flesh could not be satisfied, but who kept demanding more and still more.

When finally the overloaded trains pulled slowly out of the station, they left the platform littered with packages. Some of them had broken open and the contents had spilled out over the sooty pavement. There were books and pictures, tea cozies, slippers and embroidered pillows and other trivial objects. They were the treasures that people, torn from their homes and given only a few minutes to pack, had chosen to take from the things they had gathered together during a lifetime. Guards with brooms swept everything together into a big pile and dumped it into empty garbage cans.

On top of one of the garbage cans Elizabeth saw Bear.

When Elizabeth made her way to the first platform, the scene was very different. The express train from Germany had just come in and people were hanging out of the windows, shouting for porters. The passengers were mainly high-ranking German officers with their families, and businessmen, dressed in too new and flashy clothes. Elizabeth labeled them immediately as black marketeers or people who had dealings with the Germans. She found an empty table in the right location and watched the people pass by.

An officer and his family were walking briskly behind a porter pushing a cart full of luggage. The man and woman were talking gaily and their three boys, all in leder hosen and with green felt hats, were munching sandwiches. Another officer, his chest covered with medals, gently helped an old couple step down from the train, offered his arm and walked slowly away with them. They must be his mother and father, Elizabeth thought, and she felt a terrible anger rise inside her for those other old fathers and mothers and little children.

Elizabeth could not think of eating lunch, but she must order something to remain at the table. She took coffee, and while she drank the hot bitter liquid, she watched the hands of the clock jump convulsively from minute to minute. Altogether she had spent only an hour and a half in the hall, although it had seemed a lifetime. In less than thirty minutes she could expect to see the Cohens come up the stairs. She turned her head to make sure once more that she could really spot them from where she was sitting. At the top of the stairs stood Eva.

It was unmistakably Eva. She was lovelier than ever, wearing a navy blue coat and a little red hat on top of her blond head, with matching red gloves and handbag. For a moment Elizabeth was too stunned to think, and when she had her wits back, it was too late. Her sister had seen her and was coming toward her table.

"Elizabeth, what are you doing here?" Eva made a gesture as if she was going to embrace her sister, but Elizabeth remained firmly in her seat with the table between them. Eva hesitated, then took the opposite chair.

"I had hoped to catch Erik," Eva said when she realized Elizabeth was not going to answer her question. "I know he always comes to town on Wednesday and goes back around this time. I wanted to ask him about Father." Eva crumpled a handkerchief in her hand. "Why didn't you ever write to me again after you wrote that horrible, cold little note, telling me that Father had suffered a stroke?" Elizabeth still said nothing.

"We're leaving, the end of this week, for Italy," Eva said. "Kurt has been transferred to a military hospital there, but I couldn't leave without knowing how Father was." She stopped and stared at her sister. "Do you hear me, Elizabeth, or are you deaf?" Her voice rose as she leaned forward across the table. "I'm asking you to tell me about Father."

Elizabeth wished she were deaf. Today it would have been a blessing to be both blind and deaf. She hated Eva and her German husband with an overwhelming hatred, but worse than that she was afraid of Eva. She had no idea whether Eva could be trusted. She must get rid of her fast.

"I have nothing to say to you," Elizabeth said. "I am through with you and I hope I'll never see you again." What she had counted on happened. An angry red spread over Eva's face and neck. Without saying another word she snatched up her purse and gloves and walked away as fast as she could.

But Eva had not walked fast enough. At the moment she reached the top of the stairs two other people did too, coming from the opposite direction. Elizabeth immediately recognized Mr. Cohen and Roza, although Roza had bleached and cut her long black hair to look less Jewish.

If Eva would only turn her head some other way! Elizabeth watched with growing terror as the two came closer. Eva was walking at a brisk pace. She had passed Roza without recognizing her, and she had almost passed Mr. Cohen and was starting to go down, when she looked up. Elizabeth could not hear what she said, but she knew Eva had called out in surprise, for Roza turned back and Mr. Cohen stood still in the middle of the top step. From far away Elizabeth saw Eva kiss Roza and stretch out both hands to Mr. Cohen.

Mr. Cohen and Eva had started talking and Elizabeth, sitting on the edge of her chair, didn't know what to do. *What's he telling her?* she wondered. The train for Utrecht had come in at the far end of the platform. It was the only train they could take, for no later train would make connection with the local to Swaenenburgh. Elizabeth glanced uneasily at the clock. They had only about fifteen minutes. She shifted her glance back to the stairs.

Mr. Cohen was going toward the train now, Roza was heading in the direction of the rest rooms, and Eva was coming straight to her sister. Elizabeth braced herself.

"There's no time to talk," were Eva's first words. "Roza didn't get her papers. I'm going to give her my identity card and my coat and hat, so she'll look like me. I had my picture taken in this outfit, so she'll easily pass." Elizabeth was too dumbfounded to speak.

140

"I'm going to the ladies' room with Roza," Eva continued. "You get on the train and find Mr. Cohen's compartment." Eva had given her orders in a cool, crisp voice, showing no emotion, but now she broke down. "Why didn't you tell me why you were here?" she whispered. "What kind of monster do you think I am that you didn't dare tell me?" She turned and ran.

Elizabeth paced up and down beside the train. She couldn't go inside. There were only a few minutes left, but she had to speak to Eva. She saw Roza and Eva come out of the ladies' room. Roza was wearing Eva's coat, and the little red hat was tilted at the right angle on Roza's short, bleached hair. Eva had on Roza's shabby brown coat. She kissed Roza and waited for her to get on the train. Then without looking up or around, she walked to the exit.

"Eva, don't go yet," Elizabeth cried and she ran after her sister. In the next moment Eva's arms were around her, holding her tight. Elizabeth began to sob.

"It's all right, darling. It's all right." Eva soothed her and stroked Elizabeth's hair as she had so many times when Elizabeth had hurt herself and run to her for comfort. But Elizabeth couldn't stop. She didn't care if she was making a spectacle of herself and if people were watching. She clung to Eva. *I can't let her go*, she thought. *I've just got her back. I can't let her go right now.* She wanted to tell Eva everything and be comforted. She wanted to tell her about all the terrible, unspeakable things that she could only talk about with someone she loved very much. About the little boy, and the old rabbi who had been beaten to death, about her father and Brother Sebastiaan and her fear for Roza. But there was no time.

"You've got to go." Eva gently loosened Elizabeth's grip. "The train is leaving." She lifted Elizabeth's face. "I'll send you my address. Promise to write me every week and don't be late or I'll be sick with worry about you."

"I'll never be late," Elizabeth whispered. "Good-bye, Eva."

The train had already started when she reached Roza's and Mr. Cohen's compartment. Roza had saved the seat beside her at the window for Elizabeth. They were sisters now, according to their papers, and they could talk together. Elizabeth looked at the comfortable, soft-cushioned seats.

"Please, move over," she said in a low voice and she sat down at Roza's other side. "I don't want to sit at the window."

Chapter Nine

THERE WERE THREE PEOPLE in the compartment besides Elizabeth and the Cohens. Mr. Cohen was sitting near the door on the same side of the aisle as Elizabeth and Roza, but with empty seats between them. He was engrossed in a newspaper. To any observer he and the two girls would appear to be strangers who had nothing in common except the bench they shared during the short ride from Amsterdam to Utrecht. Although Elizabeth and Roza could talk, it was hard to keep up a natural conversation in the presence of other passengers. Roza seemed unable to talk at all. She sat huddled in her seat and every time somebody passed she jumped.

When one of the passengers casually addressed her, she murmured something inaudible and her glance shifted uneasily away. Elizabeth felt the change in Roza like a physical pain inside herself. Roza, who had always been such a brave and proud girl, wearing her star of David like a golden blazon on her old brown coat, was now like a cornered animal. Elizabeth put her hand reassuringly over Roza's.

"Take it easy," she whispered. "You've got your papers. There's nothing to be afraid of."

Roza clenched her hands in her lap. "I have a feeling that everybody is looking at me." She shrank back in her seat.

It must be clear to everybody that Roza had something to hide, Elizabeth thought, but she decided that it was wiser not to tell Roza that she was acting strange. It would only make her more self-conscious. Luckily the three other passengers, two old ladies and an old man, were too busy talking together to pay attention to Roza. If only papers weren't checked during the trip, Elizabeth thought, Roza would be all right.

Halfway between Amsterdam and Utrecht, however, the conductor came. He ordered passengers to have identity cards ready. Elizabeth's first impulse was to hide Roza in the washroom, but when she peered into the corridor, she saw that soldiers had closed off both ends of the car.

"Please, remain in your seats," an elderly soldier said to Elizabeth. "We will be with you shortly." Elizabeth could do nothing but obey. The three other passengers were chatting away and Mr. Cohen kept reading, but Elizabeth was certain he had not turned a page since they boarded the train.

"It'll be over soon," Elizabeth whispered into Roza's ear. "You're doing fine," she added.

"Your cards, please." A soldier had opened the door. He started with the three old people on the opposite bench. Elizabeth studied his back. He was a young man, big, with a thick red neck. He was very courteous and spoke in the soft singsong voice of the southern German. He looked as if he would be much more at home on a mountaintop with a herd of cows than in a soldier's uniform. He obviously did not have much experience, for he took a long time with each person. But what he lacked in experience he made up in thoroughness. He asked endless questions and insisted with firm politeness that one of the ladies take off her hat, which half covered her face. As he finished with one person and turned to the next, it became clear to Elizabeth that Roza and Eva's identity card would not hold up under his scrutiny. Mr. Cohen knew it too. He had given up any pretense of reading and was watching his daughter with anguish as the soldier came closer to her.

Now the soldier was through with the old people and

turned around. Roza was next. He stretched out his hand toward her. It was a big hand, Elizabeth noticed, with tufts of reddish brown hair growing between the knuckles of the fingers. She had not had time to think about what she was going to do, but she knew she had to do something. She leaned forward and smilingly thrust her card into his outstretched hand, before he had a chance to speak to Roza.

"You're from Bavaria," Elizabeth said in her best German. "I recognize your accent. As a child I went every summer to Garmisch-Partenkirchen. I must have climbed the Zugspitze a hundred times. It's my very favorite mountain."

"It's mine too." The young man flushed with pleasure. "We live right nearby. You must know my village." He mentioned a name that was totally unfamiliar to Elizabeth, but she nodded her head. Bavarian villages were all alike, with narrow, steep streets and dark wooden houses with geraniums in window boxes. The important thing was to keep him talking and away from Roza. She asked him questions and chattered on about her experiences in his country. She had to dig deep into her memory, for it had been a long time since she had been in Bavaria. As soon as Hitler came to power, Nicolaas had refused to set foot in Germany. What she did not remember she made up, but the soldier was satisfied with whatever she told him. He seemed to have forgotten identity cards, and when the officer in charge appeared at the door and told him to move to the next compartment he had time for only a quick, perfunctory glance at Roza's and Mr. Cohen's papers.

"It was a great privilege to talk to you," he said with typical German courtesy. *"Auf wiedersehen, Fräulein."* He smiled at Elizabeth.

"The privilege was entirely mine." Elizabeth smiled back sweetly. The influence of the Zugspitze was still so strong that he had even forgotten to say *Heil Hitler,* she observed with malicious pleasure. She leaned back against the cushions a little easier. Mr. Cohen picked up his paper and Roza, venturing out of her corner for the first time, looked out the window.

It was almost dark when they pulled into Utrecht. Their train had been delayed and they had only a few minutes to catch the train to Swaenenburgh. There was no time to look for an empty compartment and they took the first empty seats. Because of war regulations, the train was not lit and during the long, dark ride they did not talk much. People got off the train and other people got on. They moved like faceless shadows in and out of the doors. Elizabeth had hated the few times she had had to travel by night. Now, as they came closer to home, she cherished the protection the darkness gave them. To be extra safe, they got off, as planned, one station before Swaenenburgh. Erik was waiting there to take Mr. Cohen by a back road to the monastery.

The station was deserted and there was no danger in talking briefly together. Erik took Elizabeth aside.

"Major Schmidt is still in the village, having his evening beer," he reported. "You have plenty of time to get home before he does. I'll come by later."

"Good-bye, Father. Please, be careful," Roza begged.

"We'll be together soon." Mr. Cohen kissed Roza. "Don't worry."

"Father André will ring the bells for you, to tell you we've arrived safely at the monastery," Erik told Roza. "You listen for them." He took Mr. Cohen by the arm and the two men walked quickly away.

Elizabeth and Roza didn't loiter either, for they were eager to reach the woods behind Swaenenburgh. Without talking they hurried across the fields, carefully skirting the few scattered farmhouses, where a watchdog might alert people that strangers were passing by. They saw the vague shape of a bicycle rider moving on the road beyond. They lay down in the fields, pressing their bodies against the ground, and waited till he had gone on. The last stretch through the fields they ran so fast that they were out of breath when they reached the first trees.

"Roza, we're in the woods. We're safe." Elizabeth threw her arms around her friend and hugged her tight. Although the danger was not yet over, Elizabeth felt lighthearted. They were home again and these were her very own woods. Amsterdam was far away and she felt almost as if today had never happened.

"We're not quite safe yet." Roza was more cautious, but the familiar surroundings also cast their spell on her and she walked with springier steps.

Elizabeth explained that they would take the secret path. Although the soldiers hardly ever entered the woods, it did not pay to take a chance. Jacob would be waiting for them at the foot of the drawbridge. He would have checked to make sure it was safe to cross the courtyard. If he wasn't there, they were to stay in the woods until he appeared.

The secret path was not a path at all, just a trail. It ran parallel to the dirt road, but a little higher, giving a clear view of anyone who passed by below. Long ago Elizabeth, Jennie and Roza had made the secret path by marking the trees. They had spent long summer afternoons spying on Erik and Eva as they walked hand in hand along the dirt road, unaware that six eyes and six ears above them were seeing everything they did and hearing every word they spoke. But one day Erik and Eva had found out. They had been furious. Erik had given Jennie a good spanking, Eva had not spoken to Elizabeth for days, and when Jacob had heard about it, he had given the three of them a thundering lecture on respect for the privacy of others. From that day on the secret path had lain abandoned. Until now.

The woods were dark, but it was a darkness without menace. Roza remembered the way as well as Elizabeth and followed without hesitation. During the past years the path had become badly overgrown with ivy and brambles and they had to separate the branches to get through. Thorns scratched their hands and faces, and the ivy and honeysuckle caught at their hair.

"Are you hurt?" Elizabeth asked when Roza got tangled in a bramblebush. She helped free her.

"Not at all." Roza laughed and shook her blond head and that gesture brought back to Elizabeth the old Roza. With a toss of her long black hair Roza had always shrugged off every hurt or pain and she had laughed where others would have cried. *Roza will forget*, Elizabeth thought with gratitude. *In time she'll forget all the horror she has experienced during the past year in Amsterdam. Other happenings will grow over her memory, just as the brambles have grown over our secret path. And maybe I'll forget too*, she hoped. Today had not been a day she wished to remember.

Toward the edge, the woods grew thinner until they ended suddenly a few feet from the moat. Roza stood still abruptly and grabbed Elizabeth's hand. The moon was full. It shone straight into the courtyard and the four stout towers of the castle seemed to raise their pointed roofs into the sky.

"Swaenenburgh," Roza gasped. "I used to dream of this view," she said softly. "At night in bed, when I could hear the soldiers raid the ghetto, I closed my eyes and ears and pretended that I was standing right here on this spot and saw Swaenenburgh. Pinch me, Elizabeth," Roza whispered. "I'm afraid I'll wake up in a minute. I can't believe that Father and I really got away."

"You did," Elizabeth said. "Listen."

In the valley a single church bell began to peal, softly at first, but soon it was joined by all the other bells.

"Father André is ringing the bells for you."

At that very moment Roza spotted Jacob. He was sitting on a tree stump with his back toward them as he watched the courtyard. He blended in perfectly with the scenery, his gnarled body like an old oak tree. But the sight of Jacob on top of everything else was too much for Roza.

"Jacob," she choked. Jacob swung around. His glance went over the two tired, disheveled girls in front of him. It was as if the years had never passed. They were small children again. Their clothes were dirty from the fields and their hair full of twigs.

"Where the devil have you two been all this time?"

he asked gruffly. "Ive been walking up and down this blasted courtyard for God knows how long. You should have been home hours ago," he told them sternly as he had told them a hundred times when they had been little girls.

"Oh, Jacob." Roza laughed. "I'm so glad to see you." She threw her arms around Jacob's neck and kissed him.

They crossed the courtyard swiftly. Jacob had done his scouting thoroughly and there was not a soldier in sight. He unlocked the kitchen door and they stepped inside. They were home.

The kitchen of Swaenenburgh. Roza's eyes were moist as she took in the familiar surroundings and suddenly Elizabeth saw the shabby, run-down room through Roza's eyes. She was sure Roza did not notice how faded the tablecloth was, only remembered that one winter night she and Elizabeth had made the cacao stains no washing would take out completely. But Elizabeth didn't let Roza linger. She was in a hurry to get her down to the dungeon. She couldn't feel that Roza was completely safe until she had pushed the panel back into place, making the dungeon door invisible from the outside. Each of them carried a candle as they walked down the spiral staircase.

"Nothing smells quite the same as the dungeon," Roza said. "It smells of water and earth and something else." She sniffed, trying to discover the other ingredient. "I don't know what it is, but I like it," she decided.

Elizabeth didn't. She shivered. It was always cold and damp in the dungeon with a coldness that penetrated deep into your bones. The dungeon smelled of fear, she thought, but she didn't want to say it out loud. People had always been trapped in here, spending days and nights in darkness and silence. Long ago there had been the prisoners of the Barons van Swaenenburgh and recently the fugitives that her father and Jacob had hidden from the Germans, then David and now Roza. How many terrified people had the dungeon held through the centuries? Elizabeth wondered. And how many cries that had never been heard upstairs were locked within its walls? It was a hideous place, and after Roza had gone, she would never go down to the dungeon again, she promised herself. Never.

Jacob had put a little supper for them on the table. There were sandwiches and apples and a thermos flask with a warm drink.

"Look at our shadows," Roza said, taking a bite out of her apple. "You remember how they used to scare us?"

They still scared her. Elizabeth watched how the candles on the table threw forth enormous projections on the walls. With every move their shadows crawled like monsters all over the sides and ceiling of the dungeon.

"You want the last sandwich?" Roza asked. "You hardly ate a thing."

"You take it." Although Elizabeth had not eaten all day, she was not hungry. The air in the dungeon was thick and at the same time it was stuffy and cold. Roza would have to stay down here buried under the ground, Elizabeth thought. Outside, the sun would be shining and the first crisp night frosts would cover the fields, but for Roza there would be no difference between day and night or sun and rain.

"I'm going to bed," Roza interrupted Elizabeth's thoughts. She put on one of Elizabeth's nightgowns and crawled underneath the covers.

"I'll stay with you till you've fallen asleep." Elizabeth could hardly bear being in the dungeon any longer. She would have liked nothing better than to run upstairs, but to keep Roza company was the least she could do for her friend. She felt as if the walls and ceiling were closing in on her. To take her mind off herself, she began to tell Roza about the mill where she was going when she left here. Erik had told Elizabeth about Roza's hiding place.

"It's a mill in the middle of the fields. You can see for miles around. There's no chance whatsoever of an unexpected raid by the Germans."

154

"It sounds wonderful." Roza's voice was drowsy. "I'm so sleepy," she apologized. "I haven't had a whole night's sleep in so long. We never dared go to sleep for fear we'd be caught by surprise."

"That won't happen now," Elizabeth assured her. "The dungeon is about the safest place you can think of. I just wish it were not such a hole in the ground." Elizabeth looked around the dismal room. Although Jacob had brought down some books and puzzles for Roza, it remained an inhuman place to live in.

"I don't mind one bit." Roza snuggled under the covers. "Safety is a very rare luxury for a Jew these days, Elizabeth." She took Elizabeth's hand and pressed it hard, her eyes luminous with tears. "I am sure that never in my life I'll be offered a finer bedroom than the dungeon of Swaenenburgh."

As soon as Roza had fallen asleep, Elizabeth tiptoed out of the room, but when she reached the stairs, she took the steps two at a time. Upstairs she still felt as if she were choking for a breath of fresh air. She couldn't bear to remain inside to wait for Erik. She had to go out.

It was a mild night, more like spring than like fall. The autumn breeze gently swayed the trees and brought a waft of pine from the woods. Elizabeth sat down on the grassy bank and looked into the dark, murky water at her feet. With a stick she poked at a broken bottle. The moat used to be so lovely, she thought, with the water lilies and the swans. She still missed the swans and she wondered if they would ever return.

When Erik arrived a little later, he put his motorbike up against the drawbridge and sat down beside her.

"I'm glad you're still up," he said. "I was afraid you had gone to bed. Mr. Cohen told me that you saved their lives. I want you to tell me all about it and about everything else you did today."

"It was really Eva who saved Roza and so much happened to me today. Too much to tell." Elizabeth didn't want to talk about it. The day was behind her. It had been a dreadful day and she only wanted to forget.

"I'm terribly sorry, Elizabeth, that it turned out to be such a dangerous trip for you. If I had known that Roza had not got her papers, of course, I would never have sent you." Erik's voice was full of warmth and concern. "But I have good news for you," he continued cheerfully. "Roza will only have to stay here for two days. She can go to the mill earlier than we expected."

"You mean Roza will be gone the day after tomorrow?" Elizabeth was surprised at herself for not feeling a greater sense of relief. In two days the dungeon would be empty again, just as she had wanted it to be for so long. And this time it would be for good.

"Yes." Erik got up and walked over to his motorbike.

Elizabeth had not noticed it, but there was a package on the seat.

"It's from Father André." Erik put a small burlap sack in Elizabeth's lap. "He said Brother Sebastiaan would have wanted you to have it. He would have been very proud of you for what you did for Roza today."

Elizabeth untied the cord and revealed a small clump of clay with stems and leaves. There was still one perfect rose left. Brother Sebastiaan would not have been proud of her at all, Elizabeth knew with merciless honesty. Maybe she had saved Roza, but there were still a thousand Rozas left to be saved. Before her eyes came many of the faces she had seen that morning and she thought with horror how once, it seemed so long ago, she had forbidden Jacob and Erik to hide Jews in the dungeon. She had wanted to forget today, but today should never be forgotten. She fingered the soft velvety petals. She would plant Brother Sebastiaan's rose near the kitchen door and she would water it and feed it and trim it with as much care as he would have given it. She would not be a lazy gardener and in time it would cover the walls and there would be hundreds of roses.

"I don't want the dungeon empty anymore, Erik," Elizabeth said. With her hand cupped around the rose, she began to talk, slowly and awkwardly at first, for there were few words to describe what she had seen. Erik had pulled her close to him and listened intently without interrupting her. Coming to the end of what she wanted to tell him, she spoke fast, almost falling over her words. This part was easy to talk about.

"You really mean you want to continue the work your father and Jacob did?" he asked.

"Yes. Do you think it is a crazy plan?"

"No," Erik said. "It's a beautiful and courageous plan and we're desperately in need of temporary hiding places for fugitives. I only want to warn you." He frowned. "You are aware of the consequences, if we get caught?" he asked gravely.

"We won't get caught. We'll be very careful," Elizabeth said. "But if we do . . ." She hesitated momentarily before going on. "Of course, I know the consequences," she said. "Major Schmidt has spelled them out for me so many times I know them by heart. But I still want to do it."

Elizabeth looked up at Swaenenburgh. The towers of the castle seemed so strong. From where she and Erik were sitting the house loomed like an indestructible fortress. Yet this was only an illusion. It could be so easily destroyed. Like the lives of men, Elizabeth thought. About what was to happen nothing was certain. She stared down at the muddy water of the moat.

A soft ripple underneath the bridge stirred the stagnant water. As Elizabeth watched, the ripple spread wider and wider. Then seemingly from nowhere appeared two white swans. Elizabeth drew in her breath.

They were young birds, by the looks of them, and they must have hatched in spring. Their nest must be deep down in the bank of the moat underneath the drawbridge. There were low, prickly bushes that would make an excellent hiding place. Too wild and shy to come out during the daytime, when the courtyard was noisy, they ventured out only at night. Elizabeth and Erik leaned over as far as possible, afraid to make a sound that would scare them away.

Erik took Elizabeth's face in his hand and kissed her. "It's the prophecy of Frank van Swaenenburgh," he said. "You remember?" Elizabeth nodded.

"No harm will befall the castle, the monastery and the village as long as there are swans in the moat of Swaenenburgh."

About the Author

MARGARETHA SHEMIN was born in Alkmaar, a medieval town about twenty miles north of Amsterdam, Holland. During the German occupation of Holland in World War II, her father was active in the underground resistance. Many of the incidents and feelings in this book and in the author's earlier book, *The Little Riders*, are based on her own experiences.

Margaretha Shemin makes her home in Pleasantville, New York, with her husband and children.